Jean Ann's thoughts on men and dating:

36, 24, 35 only describe ages I'll never be again. So when one very handsome man who I met through the personals asked me out a second time—and a third—I was darned flattered.

Well, you know what they say about beauty. And judging books. Boy, did I learn my lesson. You see, there's this other man. The kind of man you realize you're in love with when it's too late....

Dear Reader,

Personal ads? Full of those lonely hearts looking for love in all the wrong places? *Give me a break,* some of you are probably thinking.

Granted, in Dixie Browning's *Single Female (Reluctantly) Seeks...* JeanAnn Turner dates a few doozies until she figures out where to find Mr. Wonderful. But the title of Kasey Michaels's Yours Truly novel makes a very good point: *Husbands Don't Grow on Trees.*

That, I know. I also know that if you do nothing unexpected, nothing unexpected happens. So I checked out the personals for myself. Guess what? Some very wonderful, very eligible bachelors are behind those fifty little words. All kinds, from sexy daredevils to the boy next door.

Speaking of the boy next door, isn't he supposed to be the sweet, nice type? That's what Susannah Yardley thought before she met the sexy single father next door in Kasey Michaels's *Husbands Don't Grow on Trees.* Sweet, nice types don't make you want to borrow a cup of sugar at midnight.

Next month, look for Yours Truly titles by Laurie Paige and Hayley Gardner—two new novels about unexpectedly meeting, dating and marrying Mr. Right!

Yours Truly,

Melissa Senate

Editor

Please address questions and book requests to:
Silhouette Reader Service
U.S.: 3010 Walden Ave., P.O. Box 1325, Buffalo, NY 14269
Canadian: P.O. Box 609, Fort Erie, Ont. L2A 5X3

DIXIE BROWNING

Single Female (Reluctantly) Seeks...

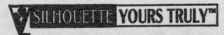

Published by Silhouette Books
America's Publisher of Contemporary Romance

SILHOUETTE BOOKS

ISBN 0-373-52007-7

SINGLE FEMALE (RELUCTANTLY) SEEKS...

Copyright © 1995 by Dixie Browning

About the author

Personal ads are nothing new. In Colonial days, planters in the New World sent all the way to England for wives. Widowers have long advertised for strong, healthy young wives to take on the burden of caring for their motherless brood. How many love stories have been spawned from just such unlikely beginnings?

But personal ads are much more exciting nowadays. Happily—*very* happily—married for forty-five years, I sometimes find myself reading them and wondering.... And then racing for the word processor to begin another new love story. The joys of love never grow old.

—Dixie Browning, on the subject of *Single Female (Reluctantly) Seeks...*

Dixie Browning has written over fifty novels for Silhouette Books. Her latest novel, *Alex and the Angel,* was September's *Man of the Month* title for Silhouette Desire *and* book one of her new Desire trilogy, Tall, Dark and Handsome. Look for book two, *The Beauty, the Beast and the Baby*, Silhouette Desire's *Man of the Month* in March '96.

Prologue

—————►◄—————

Sara took out three diet colas, popped the top on her own and shoved the others toward the two sweat-suited women perched on stools in her red-enameled kitchen. Thirst momentarily assuaged, they continued the argument. "It's for her own good. We all know Jay's getting downright stodgy."

"I wouldn't exactly call her stodgy—Jay's just satisfied with her life the way it is," C.A. argued gently.

"Satisfied with the rut she's in, you mean," Sue retorted.

"Well, it's her own rut. She made it. She obviously likes it," said Sara, who proceeded to sum up the case. "Look, Jay's going to be thirty-seven years old next Tuesday. On Wednesday she'll have been widowed for precisely ten years. Her painting is so old-fashioned, she doesn't even dare show it around these parts, and I know for a fact she hasn't had a date in seven months."

"I told you she wouldn't like that jerk you fixed her up with," reminded Sue. "They didn't even speak the same language. He was a jock, for crying out loud!"

"So?" Sara had an artist's appreciation for the male physique. As JeanAnn Turner, called Jay by her friends, was also an artist, Sara had hoped something might come of the arranged date.

Nothing had. No score. No game. Definitely no return match.

"Well, **at** least this way she'll get to screen each candidate first and see what, if anything, they have in common. If she's not interested, she doesn't have to commit herself."

"No, what she'll commit is us. She's going to kill us for this."

"What, for giving her a wake-up-and-smell-the-roses-before-it's-too-late gift? Jay knows we only want her happiness, and God knows, she can't be happy with her life the way it is. Living alone in that old mausoleum—"

"It happens to be an excellent example of the Queen Anne style of architecture," said C.A., who had taken a single course in the subject some dozen or so years earlier.

"It happens to be a white elephant," corrected Sue. "But you can't really say she's alone. What about her new boarder?"

"The professor? Talk about mausoleums, have you seen the guy?"

"He's not all *that* old. Jay says he's quiet and pays on time, and Lord knows she needs the money."

"I think he's kind of—well, you know. Good-looking."

"C.A.! Where's your taste? In those baggy old clothes—with those tacky glasses?"

"Well, I mean in an understated sort of way. I mean, he's not really bad looking. I saw him outside Wilson Library the other day and he had on a dark gray suit and a really nice tie, and—I don't know, I sort of thought—"

"Well, quit thinking, I've got a date tonight. Look, are we going to do it, or are we going to settle for taking her to dinner and a movie again?"

"Read it over again, Sara. I'm not real sure about all those abbreviations."

"All right, here goes," said Sara, sliding her square, purple-framed specs back up on her short nose. "And this time, no interruptions, please. Under the Seeking Male heading—"

"Seeking Male? That sounds more like a lioness on the prowl. Jay's a pussycat, at best."

"It's just a heading, for Pete's sake. Like Help Wanted, or Rooms For Rent. Now, simmer down and listen, will you? Okay, here goes. Body copy—37 yr old SWF—"

The kibitzing continued, one voice overlapping another. "Jay's widowed. That's not exactly the same thing as single."

"Quit nitpicking. WWF sounds like a veterans' organization. Now—where was I? SWF, interested in art, music, gardening—"

"Don't you think that makes her sound sort of...ordinary?"

Sara slapped the notepad down on the table. "Look, I love her, too, but face it—Jay's ordinary. *I'm* ordinary—we're *all* ordinary! Granted, she's sweet and smart and not bad looking, but she's never going to set the world on fire."

"So she's no arsonist—she's got nice eyes." C.A. always saw the best in everyone.

"Jay's biggest problem is that she was married to a stinker who didn't deserve her." Sue had known Ronald Turner better than the other two. "He talked her into blowing her inheritance on that old wreck of a house and then lost interest in her because she was broke."

"So? Should I have said, 'Nice eyes, was married to mercenary rat fink, has great figure but dresses like a street sweeper'? Sorry, gang, it just doesn't scan. Now, do you want me to finish reading this thing, or are you going to keep on interrupting?"

"Read on," said the coconspirators in ragged unison.

"ISO—" Sara glared over her glasses. "It means In Search Of, C.A.! ISO S/DWM, 35-45, intelligent, sense of humor, emotionally and financially secure."

"Financially secure—that makes her sound like a gold digger," ventured C.A.

"What, you want her to wind up with another deadbeat?"

"Worse still, an immature deadbeat." Sue tossed down the last of her cola. "I like it, Sara. I say we go for it."

"I've already gone for it. I turned it in before I left the office." Sara worked as a graphic artist for the *Orange County Gazette*. "Any man who reads this ad and takes the bait can call a 900 number and make his pitch. For a price—which I paid in advance, so you both owe me—all Jay has to do is call in and collect her voice mail. If she likes the sound of any of the candidates, she can call back."

"She won't play."

"She will. I fixed it."

"Sa-a-ra!"

"Okay, okay already, but you know Jay. If I hadn't rigged the system, it would never have worked. Just one of the benefits of having a little clout where it counts and being technologically literate."

"Not to mention crooked as a snake."

"Quit complaining. It'll work just fine. For the two days the ad runs, all her calls will be put through to her answering machine. She'll be out of town, and once she gets home she'll have to hear them all to clear the tape. What do you bet she'll be tempted by at least one or two? You know Jay—underneath that shy, nice-lady facade, there's a streak of recklessness a mile wide."

"Only when she's on PMS. The rest of the time, it's more like a quarter of an inch."

"Whatever. Now…who's going to call her and tell her what we've done for her?"

"Are you sure you don't mean done *to* her?"

"Trust me, we're doing her a favor. I know at least three women and two men who've met their mates and married through personal ads."

"And lived happily ever after?"

"Ever after isn't over yet. Give it a chance, you turkeys. What've we got to lose?"

1

Late Sunday-afternoon traffic was a real bummer. By the time she pulled into her big overgrown, under-groomed yard, JeanAnn Turner had a mild headache and the beginning of acid indigestion. She'd left town early Saturday morning to drive to Winston-Salem, some hour and a half away except during rush-hour traffic. The plan had been to visit her old college roommate, take in the new gallery that had recently opened, and if it leaned toward the traditional, possibly even explore the idea of trying for a one-woman show there sometime in the hazy, distant future.

After that, she had planned to drive back home and think it all over for a few more years before making any definite commitment. This unsettling urge to break out of her rut seemed to strike her about every other year, usually between March and May. Fortunately, it seldom led to anything more drastic than a change of cologne or a new shade of nail polish, which she never wore anyway, but thought perhaps some-day she might.

It hadn't taken much to convince her to stay over for the Sunday afternoon opening of a one-man show by a talented new artist. As Ollie, her old roommate, had said between dishing up spaghetti and prying the dog's bone from between the teeth of her two-year-old, it wasn't as if she had any real reason to rush back to Chapel Hill.

Which might have been downright depressing if she'd allowed herself to dwell on it.

It had been her kind of show, the works ranging from traditional to Impressionistic—nothing too far-out. Which more or less described her own style. Even though the young artist was new in town, the crowd in attendance had been good. A satisfying number of gold stars had gone up, designating first-day sales.

Jay only hoped her own show would do as well. Ollie had shown a few photos of Jay's work, which she just "happened to have" in her purse, and told the gallery manager where she had exhibited before, and in a moment of spring madness, Jay had found herself agreeing to a show in the last two weeks in November.

Now, pulling up under the carport, which had been called a porte cochere when it had been built nearly a century ago, she switched off the engine, leaned back and closed her eyes, enjoying the peaceful moment. A dog barked. A flock of linnets argued out by the bird feeder. One street over, Mr. Kolodny was playing his cello on the back porch. He practiced an hour and ten minutes every day, and Jay had come to look forward to it.

Inside her own house, the phone rang. She opened her eyes and then closed them again.

Let it ring. The answering machine, which she had finally given in and bought, would catch it. Just three minutes to unwind—that was all she asked. Every driver east of the Mississippi had decided to hit the road this weekend. The result was a bumper-to-bumper high-speed chase.

In a few minutes she would treat herself to a tubful of lukewarm, lavender-scented water, a glass of West Bend Chardonnay and the new Regency she'd picked up last week. At times like this she almost wished she'd been born in an age of curricles and carriages instead of an age of tractor trailers and demolition derbies.

This was the weekend she'd planned to get started on the yard. So much for plans. Jay liked yard work, she really did. Only there was so blooming much of it.

Eyes still closed against the late-afternoon sun, she smiled at her own pun, but the smile faded quickly. Her *eleagnus,* which was supposed to be a shrub and not a vine, was crawling up the pine tree again. The wisteria was headed up the downspout, threatening to pull down the entire gutter, which was already sagging under a load of pine straw. The yard desperately needed attention, but there was still another three weeks of school to go. By the time she got home every day, she was too tired to do more than worry about all the things she was too tired to do.

So now, on top of all that, she had committed herself to a one-woman show. No two ways about it—she was going to have to get organized. Which meant putting off this year's spring cleaning until next year, getting up at daybreak and working in the yard while it was still fairly cool and then painting like crazy until she collapsed at her easel.

And praying she turned out something worth exhibiting. When the pressure was on, her muse had a tendency to take a hike.

She sighed. For someone who prided herself on being independent, she had managed to tie herself down pretty thoroughly. The house had been a fixer-upper when they'd bought it for practically nothing during the last housing market depression. Ronnie had been full of ideas about turning it into a bed and breakfast, but like most of Ronnie's ideas, it hadn't lasted long enough to bear fruit. Jay's family was always telling her she should sell the place and move into an apartment where she could meet other people. One of these days, she might even do it.

No, she wouldn't. So she was in a rut. It was her own comfortable rut, and it would take a lot more to prod her out of it than a little overgrown shrubbery, a few clogged gutters and scores of tall windows waiting to be washed, each with dozens of panes.

The professor's pollen-covered sedan was parked under the oak tree, which reminded her that she really did need to hose off the porches before the yellow stuff infiltrated the entire house.

Somewhat surprisingly, she realized that she was glad Dr. Blanchard was at home, even though she seldom saw him except in passing. Aside from the ongoing expense, there was a lot to be said for living alone in a big, roomy house. Living alone, one could do as one pleased, with no complaints or snide remarks.

Although if she were to be perfectly honest with herself, Jay had to admit that it was rather nice to hear the occasional sound of footsteps overhead and know that she wasn't entirely alone in the world. She'd even come to enjoy hearing the sound of the professor's shortwave radio played softly late at night. There was something exotic about hearing voices from another country in the privacy of her own home.

It was about as close as she would ever come to hearing them at all, she conceded ruefully. Traveling took more money and more time than she was ever likely to possess.

Her three minutes of relaxation up, Jay slung her tote bag out onto the cracked driveway, closed the car windows to keep the pollen out and began gathering the rest of her junk. She was mentally examining the contents of her refrigerator, wishing she'd thought to pick up something on her way through town, when her renter stepped out onto the wide front porch.

Husky. It was the first word that had popped into her mind the day he'd come to look over the upstairs apartment. Tall, husky, built more like a football player than a visiting lecturer in the anthropology department at the university, Thaddeus Blanchard wore nondescript glasses on a nondescript face and baggy, nondescript clothes. At first she'd thought him dull— but then she'd begun to wonder. Once or twice she'd caught a glimpse of something—

Well, not exactly exciting, but certainly...intriguing.

And then she'd tell herself she was hallucinating. He was what he was—no more, no less. She'd come to think of him as her professor. He was quiet, with no obvious bad habits, and he'd paid three months in advance. He didn't object to the stairs, or to sharing the phone on the stair landing until she could have another line installed—which she was going to do as soon as she could save up enough to have the entire house rewired. Which was next on the list after reflashing all the fancy turrets and cupolas that looked great, but were totally impractical, and replacing a dozen or so missing slates.

Nor did he complain about the smell of turpentine that permeated the house when she switched over from watercolors to oils.

None of which could be said about her last renter, who had been a royal pain in the butt.

He came down the steps to meet her. Behind the plastic-rimmed glasses, he appeared to be scowling. He opened his mouth to speak and she noted absently that he had lovely teeth. Her late husband had spent the last of her savings account having his own teeth capped the year before he had died of a heart attack while out jogging.

"It's about time!" Blanchard snapped, which took her by surprise. They had spoken together little more than half a dozen times, but Jay had formed the impression of a quiet, courteous, soft-spoken type.

"Is anything wrong, Dr. Blanchard?"

Thad Blanchard snatched up her bag and stalked off toward the front door, and she hurried after him, juggling her purse, her keys, her sunglasses and a sheaf of papers consisting of sample invitations, notes and phone numbers, plus two quick landscape impressions she'd sketched on the backs of envelopes while waiting for traffic to move.

The phone was ringing again when she walked into the front hall. Impatiently, she dumped everything on the table and dashed up the wide, golden-oak stairs to the landing, reaching it just as the message machine cut in.

"Hell-o-oo, SWF. If you look anything like your voice sounds on your message machine, then I'm definitely interested in exploring all your interests and a few of my own. I'm 36, divorced, considered attractive, I drive a late-model sports car and art is re-a-lly my thing. In other words, I'm all the things you specified and then some. Baby, you are really in luck. Why don't you give me a call and we'll go from there?" He gave a number, but Jay, staring at the phone in open-mouthed horror, was no longer listening.

"You might have given me some warning," the professor said, his voice, for once, neither soft nor courteous.

"Where did that come from?"

"What?"

"That—that—it must have been a wrong number."

"If that was a wrong number, then half the male population of Orange County is dyslexic. The damned thing's been ringing off the wall since about two hours after you left town!"

The message light blinked rapidly. The tape whirred. Jay stared at the small black box as if it might hold a coiled cobra. Stepping back, she barged into the solid bulk of the professor, who had climbed the stairs right behind her. For a large man, he moved with surprising stealth.

"But I don't understand," she said, edging as far away as she could on the five-by-five-foot landing.

"What did you expect? Just do me a favor, will you? Next time you place an ad in the personals column, specify reply by U.S. Postal Service!"

"But I didn't place any ad," Jay wailed. Her head had been throbbing gently when she'd pulled into her driveway. Now an entire battalion of jackhammers was chipping away inside her skull.

"Right. It's all a big misunderstanding. Look, your personal life is your own business, Ms. Turner, but I'd appreciate it if you'd try to keep it a little more private from now on."

"A misunderstanding," she repeated, eyes narrowing. She squinted at the play-message button and then turned to glare at the man who was glaring right back at her. The mouth she'd hardly noticed before might have been chiseled from granite, full lower lip, curved upper one, and all. "Then I suggest you go back upstairs and cover your head with a pillow, Dr. Blanchard. If I have to stand here all night listening to this confounded gadget, I intend to get to the bottom of this—this debacle. And when I do, you can rest assured there'll be no more calls!"

Thad started upstairs, then turned back. He didn't like message machines. He didn't even particularly like telephones, preferring the timeless silence of ancient caves and windswept plains.

But then, the lady evidently wasn't any too thrilled with the results of her little venture, either—although God knows what else she'd expected. "Look, if you're all that desperate, I'll take you out myself. Anything for a little peace and quiet around here!"

Jay gawked at him. "Desperate? I'd have to be more than desperate, I'd have to be demented."

He turned and stalked off, and Jay told herself she had only imagined the fleeting look of injury that had flickered across his face.

The phone rang again. She closed her eyes, mouthed a wicked oath and reached for it before her message could cut in. After the first few words, she quietly hung up and began replaying her messages.

The clue came in the third call. And the sixth. And
the ninth. The first two were from men, stating their
credentials, some shyly, some boldly, and giving her a
number to call if she was interested. The third was
from C.A., who wondered how Jay liked her birthday present this year, and hastened to explain that it
had been Sara's idea, but she and Sue had thought it
was a good one, because after all, Jay was too young
to bury herself alive in that old mausoleum.

Mausoleum? C.A. had always claimed to love her
house!

The next two calls were in answer to the ad, and
then Sue came on to tell her that in addition to the
special "Wake-Up-and-Smell-the-Roses-Before-It's-
Too-Late" gift, she had her choice of Hungarian at
Cracovia, health food at Pyewacket or a wild and
crazy evening at 411. Their treat.

Jay swore out loud this time, with surprising thor-
oughness. She had not taught art in the public schools
all these years without learning a thing or two about
expressing herself in the modern idiom.

After that there were two more calls from men, one
of whom sounded so shy, she almost felt like calling
him back, and then Sara came on to claim full re-
sponsibility. "Jay, if you're still speaking to us, we'll
see you next Tuesday night. There won't be any re-
peat calls, and your name and address are safe as Fort
Knox. I, uh—I reckon you've already guessed this little lark was my idea. Sorry if it was a bad one. Next

year we'll treat you to a tea-tasting and cross-stitch exhibit, okay?''

By then, Jay was seated on the stairs, chin in her hand, large gray-green eyes closed. Sensing someone behind her, she said without looking up, ''That's the end of it.'' The tape was still whirring, returning to the beginning. ''Sorry you were disturbed. I'll call the paper first thing in the morning and pull the ad, just to be sure.''

''You think that'll put an end to it?''

''Lord, I hope so!''

''Don't count on it,'' he said dryly.

Thad had been ready to yank the damned phone out of the wall and tie the cords around Alexander Graham Bell's desiccated neck. His opinion of his landlady, if he'd even formed an opinion, had undergone a complete reversal. He had thought of her, when he'd thought of her at all, as a quiet, nondescript woman with a surprisingly pleasant speaking voice, a disastrous sense of style and world-class legs. He'd caught a glimpse of them one day when she was standing on a ladder, raking pine straw out of a gutter.

It had been a mistake, moving into a place like this. At the time, he'd thought ''Spacious apt, prvt hm, quiet nghbrhd,'' had sounded like just what the doctor ordered. He figured he'd earned something a bit more comfortable than the residential hotels and cheap motels he usually chose at times like this, when he was between assignments.

It was a system that worked surprisingly well. With a doctorate in physical anthropology, Thad had been able to move freely in areas where members of the Washington alphabet soup group were persona non grata. Nine years ago he had inadvertently become a vital link in the information network between such trouble spots and the State Department. Two months ago, having been caught in the cross fire of a terrorist attack, he'd been invalided home, debriefed, hospitalized and sent south under his usual academic cover to recuperate until it was time to go out again.

A loner by nature, Thad was good at his profession. Both of his professions. At forty-one, he had no family, a few good friends scattered around the globe, an ex-wife who was living at the moment in Burbank, but no close ties.

Nor did he want any. Not again.

After eighteen months in the field, he'd been ready for a break. The truth was, he was about ready to get out of the spook business altogether, only it wasn't quite that simple. As an anthropologist, he could walk across an empty field and see things that not one person in ten thousand would notice. A faint depression—a pattern of fine cracks in the soil.

And because he was trained to note imperceptible variations, he also noticed discrepancies in patterns of movement among certain groups in the areas where his work took him, which might indicate anything from small-time gunrunning, to drug-trafficking, to major conspiracies. A trained observer with sharp analytical skills and ironclad credentials, he had a professional entrée into many of the world's trouble spots, where he played a double role.

Now he wanted out. Wanted to concentrate on the profession he'd been trained for. Unfortunately, after years of having his brain tuned to a certain frequency, he was finding it damned near impossible to tune it out.

But he was working on it. For years, he'd had in the back of his mind to write a book. He'd made mental notes, organizing and reorganizing them in his spare time. Now, having moved south a month before the term began, for that particular purpose, he was finally getting them down on paper.

As advertised, the house was spacious. The neighborhood was quiet enough if one didn't count the fiddler who gave a daily concert between the hours of four and five-ten every afternoon and the sounds of his landlady's music seeping through the register in the floor of his study. Along with the smell of turpentine.

Still, he had all the privacy a man could want. The entire second floor was his. His landlady was out all day five days a week, and quiet when she was at home. Except for the music. But at least it was good music and she kept the volume down. Actually, it was a hell of a lot more restful than listening to the news on Radio Canada or the BBC and trying to figure out where he was apt to be sent next and how to get out of it.

At the moment, however, Thad was in no mood for music. Nor was he in the mood to work. Flinging off his glasses, he raked a hand through his hair. What he'd really like right now was a cold beer. Maybe a couple of beers. And a big plate of linguine with clam and garlic sauce. And maybe, to finish it off, a good cigar.

No... that wasn't what he wanted. He felt a certain kind of restlessness he hadn't felt in a long time. The kind of restlessness that could get a man into trouble if he weren't careful.

The kind that could get a woman into trouble, too.

Would his landlady's friends have placed that ad if they hadn't thought she was ripe for a little action?

What kind of action?

Hmm... Interesting thought.

No, dammit, it was *not* an interesting thought, Thad told himself. If he needed a woman now and then—and given the normal ration of testosterone, most men did—he could do a damned sight better than coming on to an old maid who looked at him as if he were something that had been pickled in formaldehyde and stashed away on a top shelf!

2

Jay fortified herself with three glasses of Chardonnay, which was two over her limit, before tackling Sara. "How could you *possibly* publish my phone number that way?"

"Jay, Jay—simmer down. Nobody published your phone number. You're a code number. Anyone reading your ad who wants to get in touch with you has to go through the paper, and it's not free. They pay three bucks a minute to be put through to your answering machine. We waited until we were sure you were going to be out of town, so if you're not interested, all you have to do is ignore the call and they'll try another ad."

"I hadn't even planned to be gone overnight!"

"Yeah, I know—we talked to Ollie."

The light dawned slowly. "Gee, thanks. With friends like mine, who needs enemies? Sara, I didn't even *have* an answering machine until a few months ago!"

"Don't I know it. Every time I tried to call, you were either at school, or outside spreading disgusting stuff around your shrubbery, or holed up in your studio at the other end of the house, with a bunch of people screeching in Italian."

"Don't change the subject. Sara, what on earth made you think—"

"You know, hon, it's people like you who're going to create all the traffic jams on the information highway. One teeny weenie little speed bump, and you fall apart. Honestly, Jay, you're a throwback to another age."

"Don't try to talk your way out of it. You set me up, and I—"

"Oops, hang on a minute, will you, hon? I've got another call."

Carefully, Jay replaced the receiver. She sat down on the step above the landing, feeling tired and discouraged and none too sure she could negotiate the eight steps down to her own floor, much less negotiate her way into a brand-new century.

A throwback.

Was she really that bad? Was she the only woman in the world who was bored instead of fascinated by technology? She had finally broken down and bought a microwave and a VCR, hadn't she? She had even learned to program the blessed thing.

Of course, no sooner had she figured it out than some technical type had come up with a way to do the whole thing by voice command, which only went to prove that there was no point in wasting your life reading manuals and learning how to use all today's high-tech gadgets when by tomorrow, they'd be obsolete, and you'd have it all to do again.

So much for her teaching degree and all those years of night classes. She still couldn't tell a microchip from a nacho, unless one of them was dipped in salsa.

She sighed. Seven steps up, a door opened silently. A whiff of cigar smoke drifted out and she drew in a deep breath, oddly comforted by a vignette of familiar memories. Her father smoked cigars. One cigar a day, after dinner, while the womenfolk cleared the table and washed dishes. By hand.

Maybe Sara was right.

Feeling as if she'd run her legs off trying to catch up with the parade, only to see the last row of marchers disappearing in the distance, Jay stood and started downstairs.

The phone rang. She swore, sighed, then retraced her steps, catching it on the third ring, before the machine could click on. "Yes, hello," she said impatiently.

"Oh. I didn't expect a real person. Is this c-c-code number B-two-oh-four?"

"No, this is not code number anything! To whom did you wish to speak?"

"I'm sorry. I was c-c-calling in answer to the ad? I, um—I'm new in town and I thought—th-that is, I studied commercial art, but I work in a b-b-bookstore now. Assistant manager. I'm afraid I d-don't know much about g-g-gardening, but I like music. I was church organist back home."

She could almost feel his sweaty palms clutching the receiver on the other end of the line. "Where's home?"

"South Carolina. Near Lake Moultrie," he said eagerly.

She sighed again and pinched the bridge of her nose. She didn't know why she'd even asked, only he'd sounded so scared. Actually, he sounded rather nice.

Sure he did. And a snake probably thought a mongoose was just another nice, warm fuzzy.

"I d-d-don't suppose you'd want to come by the store for a reading," he said apologetically, which made her wonder if she'd mistaken the intent of his call. Maybe it was just a sales pitch.

"What kind of a reading?"

"Humorous essays? Um...it's a regional writer. He's going to be at the store, and I thought it might be a n-n-nice way to g-get acquainted. B-but I guess some people would be b-b-bored. I guess you'd rather—"

"All right."

The ensuing silence quivered all the way up to the lightning rods on the turreted slate roof. Then he gasped. "You *will*?"

Jay was already regretting her momentary weakness when he said, "What about supper afterward?"

If he'd asked her out to dinner she would have said no, she told herself after agreeing to meet him at the bookstore on the following Friday night. But supper...that was different. She'd grown up on a farm in Wilkes County where dinner was eaten in the middle of the day and supper was eaten in the evening, with the whole family seated around the kitchen table. All seven of them. Mama, Daddy, Great-Aunt Ruth, two younger sisters and one older brother.

Before she could get away, the phone rang again. She answered it, still bemused by what she'd just committed herself to. Which, now that she thought about it, probably wouldn't be all that bad. At least she would have her own car if things didn't work out. She could be home safe in five minutes.

"Yes, this is B-two-oh-four." It sounded like a stock number.

"Do you have any more B-two-oh-fours left?"

"I believe we just sold the last one, but let me call the warehouse. The C-eleven is almost identical except for the whatsis on the thingamabob, but I can sell you an adapter."

By the time she came to her senses some half an hour later, reassured by the thought that by midnight tonight her ad would be a thing of the past, with no more calls directed her way, Jay was amazed to realize that she had agreed to supper and a reading on Friday night with the assistant bookstore manager; dinner on Saturday at a local Hungarian restaurant and an Irish music concert she'd been half planning on attending anyway, with a widowed insurance salesman who admitted to being one year over her stipulated age limit, but who sounded so apologetic that she'd given in.

And a movie on Sunday afternoon.

The last one had been a compromise. As the effects of the wine had worn off, most of her false courage had evaporated along with it. Most, but not all. Instead of driving all the way to Pittsboro for dinner at Fearington's with the third caller, a newly divorced dentist who had just moved to town from Milwaukee and was feeling rather lonely and sorry for himself, and then having to face the long, late drive back, she had agreed to ice cream and a matinee in town, congratulating herself on being smart enough to play it safe.

Three dates and she could forget the whole silly business and go back to working on her upcoming exhibit.

She had barely hung up the phone when Thad Blanchard emerged from his study at the head of the stairs. The study had once been a bedroom, complete with a fireplace and bay window, but raiding the used-housewares shelter at the dump, she'd found a desk, a hideous, but comfortable chair and several salvageable bookshelves.

"For a woman who claims she didn't place that ad, you surely managed to reap the benefits. What have you let yourself in for?"

The hall clock bonged nine-thirty just as the last effects of the wine dissipated like a punctured balloon, leaving her with a headache and a queasy stomach. She'd never been much of a drinker.

Or maybe it was the refreshments at the opening earlier that day, which had served as both her lunch and dinner. Something pink in a punch bowl and something brown in a tart shell.

Reaching the bottom step, she turned, gripped the newel post and assumed her most severe expression, which had never fooled her students. She didn't know why she should expect it to work on old iron face. "I *beg* your pardon."

"Have you ever done this before?"

"Done what before? Not that it's any of your—"

"Have you?"

"If you mean, have I ever gone out with a man before, I assure you—"

"A stranger."

"I was married to one for seven years."

His eyebrows lifted above the colorless plastic rims of his glasses, and Jay noticed for the first time that his brows were thick and dark and winged upward at the outer corners, lending him a slightly dangerous look. "A man, that is—not a stranger," she amended quickly.

"If you didn't place the ad, what made you say yes?" He was once again the mild-mannered professor. Jay told herself she'd been mistaken about the dangerous look. It must be the wine. Or the pollen. Or the fact that she was tired enough to sleep where she stood.

Still leaning on the newel post, she stared down at her bare feet. The knee-length denim smock she'd put on after her bath was faded and, like most of her clothes, stained with paint, but it was clean and perfectly decent. He couldn't possibly know she wore nothing underneath but a pair of French underpants.

"Why? Not that it's any of your concern, Dr. Blanchard, but I agreed to go out with the assistant manager of Bartok's Books because the poor man was so nervous, he could hardly speak. I don't think he's ever done this sort of thing before, either, so we're even."

"And the next call? I heard you say yes to him, too."

"My private calls are none of your business."

She definitely didn't imagine the dangerous note in his quietly spoken response. "Lady, for your information, I've been forced to listen to your so-called private calls all weekend long. So what did this guy have to offer? A moonlight cruise on his private yacht?"

"He offered dinner and a concert afterward. And as I happen to like Hungarian food and Irish music, I saw no reason not to accept. Does that answer your question?"

When he continued to look at her, brows winged up over the rims of his glasses, she snapped, "Well, for heaven's sake, he's not an ax murderer! He's an insurance salesman, and he apologized because he's forty-six and the ad's age maximum said forty-five, and his wife died a year and a half ago, and he doesn't quite know how to move back into the mainstream, and I felt sorry for him! What's so wrong with that?"

The professor shook his head slowly. "And the last one? There were three, weren't there? Curly, Moe and Doc?"

"Doc was a friend of Snow White's, not a stooge." Jay felt as if she were being impaled by those eyes of his. Even through lenses, they were intimidating. He crossed his arms over his chest, drawing his shirt tightly against a body that looked hard and wide.

"Oh. The dentist. Well, he sounded nice. And lonely. And he's new in town, too. And anyway, I only agreed to ice cream and a matinee just in case— Well, just in case."

The glasses slid farther down his nose and those wicked eyebrows shot upward again. "Home before dark, huh? Think that'll save you?"

The jackhammers were at it again. She pinched the bridge of her own nose. "I appreciate your concern, Dr. Blanchard, but I've been looking after myself for a number of years now. I assure you, I'm perfectly capable of screaming, gouging and kicking if it becomes necessary. I don't know what sort of people you're accustomed to associating with, but around these parts we're inclined to be fairly civilized on Sunday afternoons."

"Sure you are," he said derisively as she turned and marched off, bare heels pounding silently on the hardwood floors.

Reluctantly, Jay admitted to herself that it wasn't the first time she'd acted in haste and repented at leisure. Her mother had laughed and said she'd outgrow it. Her father, bless his big, Irish heart, had called her everything in the book, but he'd always managed to pull her out of trouble before she got in over her head. Not that she'd ever been deliberately wicked, only curious. With an unfortunate tendency to leap first and look later.

At age thirty-seven, she'd thought she'd outgrown that part of her nature. She'd certainly worked hard enough at it.

Evidently she hadn't. In a single twenty-four-hour period, she had let herself be talked into doing a one-woman show with only some seven months to get ready, and then topped it off by accepting three blind dates with three strange men. The last time she'd gone out with a man had been—

Heavens, had it been that long? The fact that her last date had been a resounding flop didn't mean she was ready to relegate her social life to the occasional night out with the girls. According to the experts, in spite of a few fine lines and a few gray hairs, a woman was just entering her prime at age thirty-seven.

Actually, the article she'd read had been discussing a woman's sexual prime, but who was she to argue with the experts?

On the other hand, when the woman in question had been widowed for ten years, when said woman lived in a university town that was overrun with far prettier, far younger women, when she had never been particularly aggressive, even in her salad days—why, then, she either lowered her standards or learned to sublimate.

Jay prided herself that her standards had grown higher rather than lower. Thus she painted and gardened. Sometimes she painted far into the night, and sometimes she gardened until every muscle in her body ached, but slowly, gradually over the years, she had built a life for herself. She was content with what she had. Friends, a home, a career. It was more than a lot of women had.

Was she lonely?

Of course she was lonely! Any woman living alone who said she wasn't lonely was either lying or deluding herself.

But she'd had her chance and blown it. Her big romance had fizzled like a wet firecracker, even before Ronnie had died. Evidently, her judgment where men were concerned was nothing to write home about. Act in haste, repent at leisure. It was the story of her life.

And now, thanks to a few well-meaning friends, she'd gone and acted in haste again.

Thad Blanchard slung his glasses across the desk and leaned back in the purple plush-covered, overstuffed chair. She was at it again. The music. The smell of turpentine.

Not that he particularly objected to either, but when he was trying to think, it was a distraction.

Face it, Blanchard, the woman herself is a distraction.

That was something he hadn't counted on. He shoved his work aside. This was Thursday. Tomorrow night he could look forward to a few hours of uninterrupted work. Ms. Turner would be out with her assistant manager, kicking up her heels at some hole-in-the-wall bookstore.

And all because the jerk was so nervous, he stuttered.

"Deliver me from a woman's logic," Thad muttered.

Women and men reasoned differently. It was that simple. Would a man go out with a woman simply because she stuttered when she was nervous?

Hell, no.

He might go out with her because she had a shapely gluteus maximus—or well-developed mammaries.

Or large, gray-green eyes set in dense black lashes.

Or a short, freckled nose and a head of thick, glossy, dark brown hair.

But not because she stuttered when she was nervous. Which only pointed out the difference between a woman's logic and a man's.

There were perhaps eighteen people in attendance at the reading, including the staff. The prose was boring, the humor a little too self-consciously Southern. Jay took her grits and greens and corn bread seriously. There was simply nothing funny about it, but she managed to smile and nod whenever her date looked to her for approval.

Sue, C.A. and Sara slipped in late and stood in the back to see how things went. Afterward they joined her while the assistant manager, whose name was Sam, and who was two years younger than she was and wore a suit and tie, although every other man in the small, musty bookstore wore jeans or khakis, saw to the details of closing up.

"Where are you two going to eat?" C.A. whispered.

"I didn't ask."

"Is that his real hair, or is he wearing a rug?" That from Sue.

"I didn't ask!"

"Well, what do you think, Jay? Will you go out with him again?"

"Saa-ra—! He hasn't even asked me!"

"I like a man who wears wire-rimmed glasses. He looks steady."

"Fine," Jay snapped. "If I want to take up skateboarding, I'll be sure to ask for his support."

"He wears a ring on his little finger. You know what they say about men who wear rings on their little fingers," Sue whispered.

"No, I don't, and I don't want to hear it. If you're silly enough to prejudge a person on any such flimsy pretext, then you're probably missing out on some wonderful experiences in life."

Sue hooted and clasped her hand over her mouth. "Ha! Look who's talking about—"

"Shh, here he comes."

The three women scurried outside, leaving Jay standing alone by the out-of-order public copy machine, feeling self-conscious and wishing she'd never gone against her better judgment.

Blind dates. At her age!

What *did* a ring on the little finger mean, anyway?

Probably that it was a family heirloom that wouldn't fit on any other finger. Sue was addicted to daytime TV talk shows. For a woman with a master's degree in English literature, she had truly lamentable tastes.

They ate at a franchise steak place, and Jay listened to the story of Sam's uneventful life and promised to tell all her friends about the upcoming readings at the bookstore. It was his idea to do something that could be publicized to get people into the store, and Jay assured him it was a brilliant one.

He mentioned a movie playing in Durham, and she told him she was working every available minute to get ready for a one-woman exhibit. By the time they parted at her car on Franklin Street, he had a gravy stain on his black knit tie and she had the beginnings of another headache.

It was the season. Pollen in the air. Sudden changes in barometric pressure.

The professor was waiting up. He had never before, to her knowledge, taken advantage of her front porch swing, and Jay wasn't particularly pleased to see him there when her headlights swung into the driveway.

The seat of his baggy khakis would be yellow, because she'd never got around to hosing off the front porch.

Nevertheless, she greeted him politely and kept right on going, through the foyer, through the front parlor, the back sitting room, the tiny backstair hall and into the kitchen, intent on taking an antiallergy pill and going to bed before her headache got any worse.

He was right behind her. "Home safe, I see. How was the reading?"

She ripped off a paper towel just in time to cover her sneeze. Three sneezes later, she said, "Fine. Just lovely, in fact. I enjoyed it enormously."

"Now why do I find that hard to believe?" he drawled. He was a Yankee. Yankees didn't drawl, but the effect was the same.

She opened the refrigerator and poured herself a glass of ice tea, started to put the pitcher back in the refrigerator and remembered her manners. "Would you care for a glass of tea?" she asked grudgingly.

"I thought you'd never ask."

"It has caffeine in it."

"I believe I can handle it," he said gravely.

Ignoring him, she tipped two capsules into her palm and swallowed them with half of her tea, then gulped down the rest. When she set her empty glass in the sink, he was still there. Watching her.

"Was there something else you wanted?" she asked.

The refrigerator compressor came on, and the quiet purr seemed to accentuate the intimacy of her delft blue and pine-paneled kitchen. In the cool glow of the overhead fluorescent light, the professor's hair looked soft and warm and tousled, his dark eyes behind the lenses uncomfortably intent.

"Something else I wanted?" he repeated. "No. I suppose not."

He told her good-night and left her standing there, wondering what had just passed between them. Because against all reason, something had. Jay would be the first to admit that she didn't know much about men, but she had a pretty fair idea that his mind hadn't been on ice tea. Or even on the sweating tumbler he'd been idly stroking with his thumb.

Oh, great snakes alive! One date and her head got so screwed up, she started imagining all sorts of crazy things!

Switching out the light, she took her headache, her itchy eyes and her clogged sinuses off to bed, where she dreamed about a big, shaggy lion with sleepy eyes behind a pair of plastic-rimmed glasses.

3

—→←—

Saturdays were special. Saturdays meant sleeping a bit later, dawdling over coffee and the *Chapel Hill News* and then choosing a chore from among the dozens waiting in line to be done.

This particular Saturday also meant that the first of her three dates was behind her. One down, two to go. That was the good news.

The bad news was that no matter where she'd happened to be working all week long, her tenant had always seemed to be somewhere in the vicinity. She'd seen more of the man in the past five days than she had in all the weeks he'd been renting her second floor. It reached the point where she couldn't seem to turn around without running in to the man.

Literally.

"Was that the mail?" he asked.

Clutching the small bundle in both hands, she turned away from the front door and barreled into his chest. "Oh, for—! I didn't hear you come downstairs."

He was still gripping her shoulders to keep her from toppling over backward, and it occurred to Jay that for all her five feet eight inches, the professor towered over her.

He favored baggy khakis and baggy white oxford cloth shirts, worn shirttail out, with rumpled collars and rolled-up sleeves. There was, however, nothing at all baggy about the body against which he was holding her.

She blinked, caught her breath and stepped back, and was faintly disappointed when he let her go so quickly. If she'd suspected it before, she was no longer in any doubt that this year's version of spring fever was a particularly virulent strain. How else could she explain having agreed to do a one-woman show in little more than seven months' time, accepting three blind dates in a row and now this? Lusting after a mild-mannered professor who probably wouldn't recognize desire unless it had a Latin name and was listed in an appendix in some dusty, ten-pound tome.

"Oh, I— Let me go through this stuff and I'll— Here, this one's yours." Flustered and untidy from having just hosed off the front porch, she was amused at her own gaucherie. Really, you'd think she was some impressionable fifteen-year-old schoolgirl instead of a middle-aged widow.

"Yours," she said, handing him a pale blue envelope addressed in a backhand rife with flourishes and curlicues. "Looks like the rest is mine. Junk mail, mostly. Would you like a few catalogs?"

What would he make of Victoria's Secret? Not even her best friends knew about that particular weakness.

Sorting through the small bundle, she tossed most of the catalogs in the wastebasket, tucked the utility bill into her pocket and carried Victoria's Secret and two seed catalogs back to the kitchen to read over her lunch.

"So tonight's the insurance salesman, right? Dinner and a concert?" the professor asked from a few feet behind her.

Startled, Jay yelped and dropped the catalogs, which the professor picked up. She nodded and grabbed two mugs, which she filled with coffee, then took out a carton of milk and a plate of cold shepherd's pies. "Sugar?" she asked.

His brows slanted upward, his glasses slid down a notch and then he shook his head. "No thanks."

She nibbled the crust of one of the meat pies. Thad helped himself and bit into another one.

"These things are good!" He took another bite, and Jay enjoyed another glimpse of his nice square teeth.

He had nice square hands, too. Large, but well formed. Her last renter had been a mathematics professor in his late fifties. He'd had the hands of a child—smooth, delicate, with tiny pink nails on short, tapered fingers.

Thad Blanchard had the hands of a well-scrubbed laborer. It occurred to her that a man's hands revealed a lot about his character and personality. The trouble was, she didn't quite know how to interpret the evidence. With an artist's eye, she mentally estimated the width of his shoulders. Impressive!

He helped himself to another meat pie, and Jay thought it was just as well she was going out for dinner tonight. Then, as if he'd read her thoughts, he said, "Figured you wouldn't want to ruin your appetite."

She wanted to tell him it was none of his business, but it went against the grain to be rude. She'd been taught good manners. Didn't always use them, but she'd been taught. "I'll probably be late, but I'll try not to disturb you when I come in."

Thad had a feeling he was going to be disturbed, no matter how quiet she was, but that was his problem, not hers. Having finished the third cup of coffee, which was weak for his taste, and having polished off three meat pies, which were crisp, tender and surprisingly well seasoned, he shoved back his chair and stood. "No problem. I usually read well into the night. Thanks for the snack, Ms. Turner."

Jay stared after him in amused consternation. Half a pot of coffee and three shepherd's pies was a *snack?* For her, it would've been a meal and a half. But then, Professor Thaddeus Blanchard was a big man.

A big and surprisingly attractive man.

She wore a pink-and-gray floral print with what her mother called a Bertha gracing the neckline. Sue would have approved. Sue was into retro dressing. Her mother had practically wept when she'd seen it, claiming to have worn a dress almost exactly like it the day her Leo had proposed to her.

Leo was Daddy. Her parents were still embarrassingly affectionate after more than forty years of marriage, which made Jay all the more conscious of her own dismal failure. With such a splendid example to go by, one would have thought she'd know better than to marry the first good-looking guy to sweet-talk her into his bed.

She finished brushing her hair, which was long and thick—nearly black, but not quite—and pinned it into a wad on the back of her head. After fluffing the fringe that covered her high forehead, she fingered on a touch of lipstick, sprayed a whiff of cologne into the air and walked through it, then collected her crocheted handbag, which was too small to be practical but looked nice with her outfit.

Her professor was standing on the stair landing overlooking the front door when the doorbell rang. He was holding the phone in his hand, although he didn't seem to be talking.

Jay nodded politely, turned her back on him and opened the door. "Oh, hi," she said breathlessly to the tall, attractive man in a new haircut and an impeccably cut navy blazer. "I'm JeanAnn Turner, and you're Bob—?"

"Haverty. It's a real pleasure to meet you, JeanAnn. I must say I'm grateful to you for taking pity on a lonely widower who's new in town. And to find out you look as lovely as you sound is—"

The door closed behind them. Halfway up the stairs, Thad voiced his opinion. "JeanAnn," he muttered sarcastically as he stomped back upstairs, trying to ignore the faint drift of a cool floral scent that reminded him of a garden half a world away, where he'd once enjoyed a brief encounter with a lovely woman who, as it later turned out, did a thriving business in stolen artifacts.

Bob talked about his late wife over drinks. Over salad, he talked about the house they'd been buying. Over the entrée he talked about his work, and over dessert he regaled her with his various efforts to reenter the dating game via singles' clubs, singles' bars, church groups and the endeavors of well-meaning friends.

"Nobody really clicked. You know what I mean—chemistry? I mean, even for a nonintimate relationship, you need some sort of chemistry, don't you?"

Jay nodded, knowing exactly what he meant, but not wanting to discuss it. She was a long way away from any intimate relationship. Miles and miles away.

Unbidden, the image of her professor drifted into focus, and she forcibly pulled her mind back to what her date was saying.

Which was more of the same. The difficulty of finding a date for business social functions. Being sent by his firm to a conference in Honolulu and told to invite a guest, and having no one to share the spoils.

He had a pleasant speaking voice, which was a good thing, because by the time they reached the place where the concert was to be held, Jay had heard more than she really cared to hear about the life and times of Robert Taylor Haverty.

"Lovely," she said when he asked her opinion of the seats. He was really rather good-looking, his manners were impeccable, but it was the first time all evening he'd asked her opinion of anything.

The Irish group was rowdy and talented. An aficionada of the genre, Jay recognized most of the selections.

"Too bawdy for my tastes," said Bob as they shuffled out two hours later after five encores. "I prefer lyrics I can understand."

If you couldn't understand them, how do you know they're bawdy, she wanted to ask but didn't. The evening was almost over and she'd just as soon end it on a peaceful note. All she wanted was to get home, get out of her panty hose, which kept creeping down, and unpin her hair, which also kept creeping down.

"Would you like to go somewhere for a drink?" he asked, and she declined hurriedly, hoping he wasn't going to insist.

"It's been lovely, but I have to get up early tomorrow—"

"Another time?"

She murmured something noncommittal as she folded herself into his expensive late model car. They were both silent on the way home, knowing the relationship, such as it was, was going nowhere. No chemistry.

Jay could have told Sara right up front that it wasn't going to work. *Would* have told her if she'd been given a chance. It was just that they were all three happily involved—Sue and Sara with long-standing affairs and C.A. with her husband, and they were all quite sure she was miserable without a man of her own.

Jay kept trying to assure them she was perfectly happy with her life just as it was.

Or, if *happy* was too strong a word, then certainly content.

Bob walked her to the door. Smiling, they each murmured a few polite banalities, and then Jay waited, still smiling, for him to back out of her driveway before she let herself in, closed the door, leaned against it and sighed. He hadn't tried to kiss her. She hadn't expected him to.

"That bad, hmm?"

Startled, she dropped her purse, spilling the contents on the floor. Thad came down the few remaining steps and knelt to help her gather them up. A lipstick, a handkerchief, two safety pins and a Band-Aid in case of emergency, a roll of breath mints and a coin purse with her mad money inside.

He picked up the breath mints, which had rolled under the hall table, tossed them in his hand twice and grinned. "Didn't you need 'em?"

"Need what?" she snapped.

"Didn't he even kiss you good-night?"

Tightening her lips, she reached for the key ring she'd dropped when she'd knelt to gather up her belongings, furious because he always seemed to catch her at a disadvantage.

"Good policy," said Thad with a sagacious nod. "These days, getting physical too soon can be a mistake."

"If you're in for the night," she snapped, withering him with a look, "I'll lock up."

Clutching her lumpy purse, she twisted around to the door and flipped the night latch, then stalked off, her pink-and-gray-floral-clad back stiff as a broom handle.

"Good night, Ms. Turner," Thad called softly after her. She could tell he was grinning from the sound of his voice, and she ground her teeth.

A man of his age! A professor of anthropology! Heaven knows, she didn't have a particularly high opinion of the male of the species, but she'd expected better of a man of his stature than any such sophomoric taunts.

Two down and one to go.

After a restless night, Jay woke on Sunday morning just as the sky was brightening. Unable to go back to sleep, she dragged herself from bed and stumbled into the shower. It promised to be a perfect spring day. Perversely, she almost wished it were gray and rainy. It would suit her mood better.

A little while later she stood before her easel and squinted at the amorphous landscape loosely sketched in with strokes of turpentine-thinned raw umber. If she could just get into a painting, she could lose herself for the rest of the day and forget dating games, forget her meddlesome tenant—forget even the self-imposed pressure of painting for a show.

She would need at least fifteen midsize canvases, with two or three large verticals to anchor the walls. And if that rationale for painting was more pragmatic than aesthetic, so be it. With a living to make, she couldn't afford *not* to consider practicalities.

After a while she turned on her music. Fresh drips of raw umber turpentine wash appeared on her smock, a streak of thalo blue on the side of her nose. The composition began to take shape as she blocked in the dark shapes of trees and muddy foreground against the paler shades of sky and reflective pond. Perhaps movement might be suggested later by a flock of pigeons, light against dark, dark against light...

One floor above the studio, Thad struggled to concentrate on a section of notes concerning the modern application of his particular specialty, which happened to be the discovery, the recovery and the analysis of ancient skeletal remains, including the extrapolation of the circumstances of the demise.

On more than one occasion he'd been called in to help some law-enforcement agency discover, recover and analyze the remains of a victim of crime. Although he'd written two articles on the topic, he had not yet decided whether to include those particular experiences in his current project.

Forcing himself to ignore the strong smell of turpentine rising from the floor register beside his desk, he scribbled a few more notes in his all-but-illegible handwriting. Then, scowling, he raked back his chair and shoved his glasses up onto his head.

Thad seldom had trouble sleeping. Last night he'd lain awake for hours. As a result, he'd woken up later than usual this morning, feeling thickheaded and irritable. He'd made himself a pot of coffee in the minuscule kitchenette and been half tempted to go downstairs and see if he could talk his landlady out of her last cold meat pie.

But he hadn't. Black coffee and turpentine didn't sit well on an empty stomach. It didn't help that she'd fried bacon for her own breakfast, the mouth-watering aroma mingling with the lingering smell of turpentine.

Dammit, it was almost as distracting as that perfume she'd been wearing last night. The tantalizing fragrance had followed him into a troubled dream when he'd finally fallen asleep, triggering memories of a certain garden, and of the woman he had walked with in that garden—a woman who had existed only in his mind.

Which was a sure sign that his brain needed an overhaul.

Her name had been Angelique. In looks, she'd been the exact opposite of his ex-wife, which was a point in her favor. Bowled over by her delicate blond beauty, Thad had seen exactly what he'd wanted to see.

Which was exactly what she'd intended him to see. Beauty, intelligence, integrity and an unconscious sensuality. Of course, he'd realized that she'd lacked a sense of humor—one attribute that was impossible to fake. Even so, it hadn't been long before he'd started making plans. Long-term plans. Which had come as something of a shock, as he had long since sworn off anything of that nature.

Angelique had looked at him and seen exactly what she'd wanted to see, too.

A dupe.

A means of getting onto a restricted site and subverting a few of his native helpers with a promise of cash on the barrelhead for every marketable artifact they could smuggle out.

It hadn't helped that he'd been playing a double game, himself, uncovering information on her brother, who'd been a major player in the arms smuggling business.

Once he'd discovered her game, he'd wound up his business there as quickly as possible, sending his information about her brother through the established channels and then tipping off the museum authorities about Angelique's profitable sideline.

He had felt lousy about turning her in. Guilty as hell. Under the circumstances, he'd had no choice.

What she'd been doing had been not only criminal but irredeemably destructive.

For years afterward, painfully aware of his flawed judgment where women were concerned, he'd steered clear of all but the most transitory relationships. Any fool with half a brain should have known that when a woman as beautiful and as desirable as Angelique went out of her way to seduce an anthropologist, there had to be a catch. But he'd just come off a long, dry spell, and besides, he'd been so damned flattered—

So his hormones had kicked in and his brain had shut down, and for a few memorable nights he'd shut his mind to the fact that women like Angelique were too rich for the blood of any dusty old anthropologist. Too rich for the blood of any kid who'd been left homeless at the age of eleven, run away from two foster homes by the time he was eleven and a half, earned his GED in reform school, where he'd learned enough about gambling to finance a college education, gone through a miserable short-term marriage and an even more miserable divorce.

Too rich, not to mention too dangerous.

Now, tossing his pen down onto his notes, Thad stood, stretched and crossed to the window. Morosely, he stared down on the sprawling, unkempt shrubbery that threatened to envelop a small outbuilding at the end of a grass-shrouded flagstone walk. A rake and a stack of clay pots outside indicated that the place was a potting shed of some sort.

He should have known better than to move into a place like this. A guy could get involved without even realizing it—especially a guy who'd spent most of his life in tents, dormitories or barracks of one kind or another.

There was a solid feeling about a house like this—the kind of feeling that could trap an unwary man into thinking in terms of permanent commitments.

Luckily, he'd already been vaccinated.

The phone rang. Thad waited to see if his landlady would catch it. When she didn't, he let the machine take it.

It was her matinee date, telling her he had two tickets for a concert for Wednesday night if she was interested.

Why waste three bucks to go through the operator just to tell her something he could tell her in person? The guy would be picking her up in a couple of hours.

Thad muttered a few mild oaths and told himself he was irritated at having his concentration broken, ignoring the fact that he hadn't been able to concentrate all morning.

Prowling the room, he bent over the floor register. He couldn't see what she was working on, but through the grill he could see a foreshortened view of her body. Glossy dark head, small square shoulders, small round breasts and bare toes.

Either she had an itch that needed scratching, or she was dancing. A stroke, a little whirl. Another stroke and a satisfied little shimmy. He grinned. Apparently, her work was going well. He wished he could say the same about his own.

Standing over the register, he watched, fascinated, as his landlady continued to dance and paint to the lugubrious strains of an Italian opera. He was half tempted to go downstairs for a closer look.

No, he wasn't. Dammit, what he really wanted to do was to shut out the noise and the damned smell so he could concentrate on his own work.

He kicked impotently at the lever on the ancient register, cursed its lack of cooperation and slung himself back onto his desk chair.

Three minutes later there was a sharp rap on his door.

"Go away," he growled, knowing even before she stuck her untidy head into his study who his visitor was and and why she was there.

"I'm sorry if the music disturbed you, Professor. All you had to do was tell me and I'd have turned it off."

"Does that go for the smell?"

"The smell?"

"The whole house reeks worse than a naval stores depot."

She looked so perplexed, he almost relented. No woman whose hair looked like a squirrel's nest, whose nose had not only a peppering of freckles, but a smear of blue paint, whose big gray-green eyes had dark, half-moon shadows underneath—no woman who looked like that had any business looking so damned appealing.

"Turpentine," he muttered. "Forget it. I'll just keep the register closed." If he could have closed the thing, he damned well would've. Which she had to know.

"I'm sorry. I should have tried harder to close it once I stopped using the furnace, but it doesn't work very well anymore. Maybe a new filter—or a rug. I might even have something in the attic I could—"

"I said forget it!" he snapped, wishing she didn't look quite so much like a puppy who'd been kicked off a dry porch into a cold rain.

"I'll take care of it right away."

"Ahh—! Look, I'm sorry I mentioned it, okay?" Angry for no reason at all—which made him even angrier—Thad reached for a Cuban Double Corona from the box sent to him by a colleague in Canada. He made a production of lighting up and blowing a stream of smoke in her direction. "There. We're even now."

She stiffened. Looking martyred, offended and dignified all at once, she turned and left, closing the door quietly behind her.

He wished to hell she'd slammed it. Preferably on his neck. That had been not only inconsiderate, it was close to unforgivable. He had his faults—more than he cared to recount—but as a rule, deliberate rudeness wasn't among them.

Back in her studio, Jay glared at the ceiling as she quickly washed her brushes in turpentine, then in soap and warm water. She covered her palette, stacked her miscellaneous sketches and glanced around the room that had once held Ronnie's workout equipment. He'd been into bodybuilding. Rain or shine, he'd jogged five miles a day through downtown traffic. He'd been right in the middle of the 400 block of Rosemary Street when he'd had a heart attack.

Jay had been devastated. By then, her rose-colored glasses had long since been broken, but Ronnie had been her husband, after all. Besides, he'd been too young to die that way. Aside from his running regimen, he'd belonged to a gym and a pool. In fact, aside from an unfortunate taste for junk food and beer, he had spent more time and money looking after his health during the seven years of their marriage than she had in her entire lifetime.

But then, she'd been too busy trying to keep up with a job and renovations on the house and grounds, not to mention trying to hang on to whatever financial security they had, to spare any time for jogging or working out.

As soon as she'd gotten over the shock of her young husband's death and dealt with all the details of debts—he'd had a shocking number of those—and insurance—he'd dropped the premiums and the policy had lapsed—Jay had sold his equipment, using the money to have a new hot-water heater and sump pump installed in the basement, which had a tendency to flood during heavy rains. After that she had moved her studio out of the dark, hot attic and into this large, multiwindowed room.

So now she would move again.

Only first, she had an appointment with a dentist.

4

—▸◂—

"Bones have a story to tell," Thad wrote. "Age, sex, race, life-style—it's all there, spelled out for a discerning eye to read a year or even fifty thousand years later."

Outside the open window, a car door slammed. He heard laughter and two sets of footsteps crossing the broad front porch. The insurance salesman hadn't made it as far as the front door. The bookstore manager hadn't even made it as far as the right street.

And then he heard voices from the foyer. She'd invited him inside?

That was her problem and not his, Thad reminded himself. Only, what if the guy turned out to be a creep? She didn't even know him. He was a voice on the phone. He'd read her ad, paid his money and been put through to her answering machine, and she'd agreed to go out with him.

Which meant only that he was marginally literate, marginally solvent and too damn convincing. He could still be a creep.

Thank God this whole foolish business was about over. He would just as soon be able to get back to normal.

Placing a petrified *harpactocarpinus* on his notes as a paperweight, he stood, stretched and wandered over to the door, which he opened—to make sure he'd hear if his landlady screamed.

From the kitchen came the sound of ice cubes being dumped into a glass. A little silence, and then the sound of laughter echoed through the house. Hers was a throaty giggle—infectious.

The guy's was more like a braying jackass.

The smell of wisteria drifted through the open front door, along with a faint cloud of pollen, reminding Thad that he'd been planning to hose the yellow stuff off his car. He figured he might as well do her car at the same time. And he might as well do it now. The forecast hadn't called for rain tonight. As a scientist, he trusted weathermen only marginally more than he trusted tea leaves. But as a guy whose carcass had taken more than a few hard knocks over the years, he had learned to trust his bones.

It was going to rain. But what the devil?

He took the back stairs, which were steep, narrow and poorly lighted, but which led to the side door nearest the outside faucet.

They also happened to end up about eighteen inches from the kitchen door.

On his way out, he just happened to glance through the doorway as his landlady set out a plate containing the last leftover meat pie.

"Oh, Professor—did you want something?" Her cheeks were flushed, her eyes sparkling. She looked ten years younger, which would put her age at about fifteen, he figured. To his forty-one.

Oh, hell.

"I thought I'd rinse off my car. Want me to do yours, too?"

"Oh, please—I mean, if you don't mind? I'd planned to do it this weekend, but everything's been so hectic."

Thad regarded the good-looking jerk in pink slacks and a madras shirt. Yeah. My, how time flies when we're having fun, he thought sourly, and then wondered what the devil had happened to his objectivity. Certain of his instincts had been honed to a fine edge over the years. Even so, he'd never been one to make snap judgments. Especially when he had no more to go on than a pair of pink pants and a purple plaid shirt.

"I'll hose it down and do the porch, too, while I'm at it," he said to make up for his churlishness.

"Dr. Blanchard, this is Dr. Weems. We're going to an outdoor sculpture exhibit as soon as I get a shawl." She was flushed and flustered. The male model type looked smug. "Oh, and I might be late again tonight," she caroled after him.

Thad was halfway out the door, but he turned with a sweet-nasty smile and said, "Not too late, I hope. Remember, Jay, you have school tomorrow."

Jay? she marveled as she watched him disappear out the back door. Where had that come from? No one called her Jay except for her family, her neighbors and her friends, none of whom he'd even met.

That blasted answering machine. One of these days...

Jay still couldn't believe her luck. Mike Weems was a living, breathing hunk! He was also excellent company. She couldn't imagine why he'd even bothered with the personals ads, but she'd never been one to look a gift horse in the mouth.

The exhibit-goers, garbed in everything from jeans to georgette, seemed determined to have a good time, in spite of the occasional rumble of thunder. Spotlighted among the weeping cherry trees and the formal box hedges, the pink dogwoods, golden keria, white lilacs and beds of colorful tulips, was a collection of stone and metal garden sculptures—some grotesque, some merely whimsical.

As student waiters kept the guests supplied with an assortment of refreshments, and a string quartet played quietly in the background, several couples played croquet. The wife of a prominent pediatrician was wading in the koi pool, wineglass in hand, and Jay wondered why she had wasted ten years when she could have been doing this sort of thing all along.

Am I having a wonderful time?

Well, of course I'm having a wonderful time! What woman in her right mind wouldn't be having a wonderful time?

Then why did she feel like such an imposter?

Mike slid an arm around her waist. It fell away when she leaned forward and peered at the discreet sign at the base of an eight-foot-tall construction of copper and brass. "I can't read it. Do you suppose it's a praying mantis?" she asked, wishing she dared take off her shoes and wriggle her toes.

"Either that or a Jules Verne helicopter—I'm not sure which." He placed a hand on her shoulder just as she turned aside to wave to someone she knew slightly from school.

Intimate relationships. Bob had talked about them last night. Thad had hinted at the dangers of getting too physical too quickly. She certainly wasn't ready for anything like that. At the rate she was going, she might never be, although that was a depressing thought, too.

"Penny for 'em," Mike whispered, so close to her ear, she shivered and jerked away.

"Oh, I— Nothing." And then, because she was basically an honest person, she said, "I was just thinking that managing any kind of a social life once you've been out of the running for a few years isn't easy."

"Especially not now," he said, and Jay didn't have to ask what he meant.

Did Thad Blanchard have a social life? The thought came out of nowhere, taking her by surprise. She'd seen no indication of one. He ate take-out suppers alone in his study, made coffee and whatever else he consumed alone in his kitchenette, and worked around the clock so far as she could tell on some secret project. If he'd been a chemist, she might have worried.

Was he married? Widowed? Divorced? Uninterested?

"Another penny?" Mike teased, his slightly garlicky breath stirring tendrils of hair on her cheek. Jay had stuck with the stuffed grape leaves and the raw vegetables and dip, declining the sushi and the snails impaled on frilly toothpicks. Dr. Weems was evidently more adventurous.

"You're going to run out of pennies," she said with a laugh. "That tall piece of rusty iron sculpture..." she said, nodding to a piece on the other side of the pond. "What do you suppose it represents? A giant cobra rising up out of a potato basket or a rocket balanced on two barrels of rocket fuel?"

Looping an arm around her neck, Mike chuckled. "The catalog calls it Winged Eros. I leave it to your imagination, darling."

Jay felt as if she'd swallowed that last stuffed grape leaf whole. Fanning herself with her catalog, she turned to what was unmistakably a gigantic sunflower and muttered something about the possibility of rain.

Fortunately, the thunder was getting closer, which justified cutting the evening short.

Even so, she felt a vague sense of disappointment. Mike Weems was all any woman could want in an escort. He was certainly handsome enough. She would've had to be blind not to be aware of the way other women's eyes had followed him all evening long. Two women had waved and called him by name— neither of them particularly young or pretty. She wouldn't have thought they were his type.

But then, she wouldn't have thought she was, either. He was younger than she was, for one thing. And much more attractive.

Still, he was good company, knowing a little bit about a lot of things so that conversation never lapsed. His manners were excellent and he didn't talk about his ex-wife all the time the way Bob Haverty did. On a scale of one to ten, he was probably an eleven.

Which left her with just two questions.

Why would such a man need a dating service?

And why on earth did she keep seeing, instead of a handsome, curly-haired Adonis in expensive sports clothes and European shoes, a shaggy professor wearing nondescript clothes and glasses that kept sliding down his meddlesome nose to reveal a pair of wickedly mocking eyes?

Sara, Sue and C.A. were right. When it came to men, she was a washout.

She had left the porch light on, and the one in the foyer. The soft glow of a light from the bay window upstairs spilled out over the mock orange bush and the overgrown flagstone walk that led around the side of the house.

He was still awake.

"I really think we ought to do this again, don't you?" Mike suggested softly. He had the kind of voice that could sell water wings in the Gobi Desert.

"Oh, I—well, that is, I—"

"Wednesday night? The chamber concert I mentioned?"

They were standing in the foyer. Jay had said goodnight to him at the door, but he'd pretended not to hear her and followed her inside.

Now she glanced nervously at the front stairs, halfway expecting to see the professor appear on the landing. "Wednesday?"

"Pick you up at seven, right? And, Jeannie—if I can get away tomorrow night, why don't we drive over to Durham to—"

"Oh, Mike, I'm not sure—"

"No problem. I'll call you tomorrow." His voice had that soft, deep, sincere sound again—the one that put her instinctively on guard, which was why his kiss landed on one side of her nose instead of her mouth.

He laughed ruefully, but Jay could tell he wasn't particularly amused. She was no expert, but she knew enough about men to suspect that he'd been hoping for a little more than a nightcap when he'd followed her into the house.

"Mike," she asked, frowning, "how long did you say you've been divorced?"

"I didn't. But if it matters, since the last day of February."

"A year ago?"

"A month and a half ago," he corrected with a self-mocking smile.

"Do you mind if I ask you something?"

"You just did."

"Yes, but—well, look at you." She did. He was handsome, suave, good company—the kind of man most women would grab in a minute. "Why on earth did you ask me out?"

He had a nice laugh, but at times it was a little too practiced. His gaze strayed to her modest bosom and lingered a few seconds before slowly making its way back up to her face. "Why? Why not? After reading your ad I felt as if I knew you better than I knew my ex-wife, and I'd known her since our kindergarten days."

Jay pursed her lips in a silent O. It made sense...sort of, she supposed. "Cards on the table, you mean," she murmured.

"Cards on the table." He smiled again. His smile was totally disarming, but Jay found her thoughts straying. She wondered idly what kind of a hand Thad Blanchard was holding.

Or if he even played the game.

Distracted, she found herself agreeing to attend the concert with Mike on Wednesday night. "Pick you up at seven," he reminded her. "We'll have dinner first."

Jay nodded weakly, saw him out and closed the door, then leaned her forehead against the cool beveled glass. All her instincts told her she was playing out of her league. If Mike was an eleven, using the same scale, she was at best a five. So why, after having spent the better part of ten hours with her, was he still interested? He could easily have found any number of women both younger and better looking to go out with.

On the telephone, he hadn't sounded particularly handsome. He'd told her he was new in town, and newly divorced, and she'd felt sorry for him. She'd always had a thing for stray animals.

Ha! The day a hunk like Mike Weems needed her sympathy was the day she entered a Miss Universe pageant.

"I've got a fresh pot of coffee and some cold pizza if you're interested," said a familiar voice from somewhere overhead.

It was almost as if she'd been waiting. With a sense of fatalism bordering on relief, Jay turned away from the door and looked up at her reassuringly ordinary tenant. "Sounds like a sure recipe for nightmares," she said with a reluctant grin.

"Who wants dull dreams? Your place or mine?"

"Yours reeks of cigar smoke."

"Yours reeks of turpentine," he shot back with a smile that took the sting out of his words. "You look like your feet hurt. Go get into something comfortable, I'll be right down."

It was a quarter of eleven. She'd meant to get up half an hour early in order to run the vacuum before she left for school, seeing as how she hadn't done a lick of housework all week, but she was too wound up to sleep. Wound up, worn out and confused. If Sue or Sara or C.A. could have seen her tonight, they'd have still been smirking and congratulating themselves for Mike Weems. One out of three wasn't bad. Actually, none of the three had been losers.

So why wasn't she thrilled?

She wandered back to her room, absently unpinning her hair and giving her scalp a good scratch where the hairpins had dug in. She stepped out of her black patent sling backs, peeled off her panty hose, hung up her yellow linen and sighed. It was great to be home.

Not that she hadn't occasionally missed going out with a man, but dating was a hassle. She always felt as if she had to be on her best behavior, which made relaxation impossible. After Ronnie, she could never quite bring herself to let down her guard.

By the time she entered the kitchen, wearing a batiked caftan that was only a little bit paint stained, the professor was there, taking out cups and nuking the pizza.

"I didn't ask, but maybe you'd rather have it cold?" he said.

When he looked up suddenly like that, his glasses slid down his nose, and Jay thought it was a crime to hide such beautiful eyes. They were dark—either brown or dark hazel. She couldn't be sure in the harsh overhead light. But tonight they looked gentle and thoughtful. And at the moment, gentle and thoughtful seemed like the two most desirable qualities in the world.

Dropping down onto one of the mule-eared chairs, she sighed. "You choose. I don't want to have to make a single decision for the next eight hours."

It was funny, the way they eased into it. Later, Jay told herself it was only because she'd been tired from the constant strain of being with a stranger for so long, of trying so hard to make a good impression. Ever since she'd been a child, being on her best behavior for any length of time had been an onerous chore. Which was probably why she'd gotten into so much trouble once the parental pressure was off.

Thad—he'd asked her to call him that, and because Dr. Blanchard was such a mouthful, she obliged— fixed her coffee the way he'd seen her fix it before, and she appreciated it all out of proportion to the simple task.

I mean, really, JeanAnn, how hard is it to add two teaspoons of sugar and a dollop of cream?

He dutifully picked the anchovies off her slice of pizza when he saw the dubious way she was looking at them, and added them to his own.

She sipped her coffee. It was hot, fresh and delicious—a lot more to her taste than the astringent wine served at the garden exhibit. Chin propped in her hand, elbow on the table, Jay smiled sleepily.

"Tired?" he asked, his voice a gentle rumble that was, oddly enough, not at all intimidating.

"Mmm. I'd forgotten how tiresome it is, going out and having a wonderful time."

His nice, square-palmed hand paused momentarily on the way to his face with a slice of pizza. "You're going out with him again?"

"Wednesday night. A concert. He said he called, but I guess I forgot to listen to my messages."

They ate without further conversation, and then Jay leaned back in her chair, shoulders slumped. Tomorrow was Monday. Back to school, home again, and with what little energy she could summon up, she would start cleaning out the potting shed to move her studio out of the house. It would be better than smelling up the house. The potting shed wasn't very large, and the lighting was lousy, but she could always paint outdoors, weather permitting.

At least she wouldn't be subjected to any more complaints about the smell of turpentine. If even the mild-mannered professor mentioned it, it must be worse than she thought, and she couldn't afford to alienate a tenant. Not with taxes and utility bills to pay and a leaky slate roof that would cost a fortune to repair.

It thundered during the night, and her classes were more hectic than usual. No one, not even her most devoted students, seemed interested in beginning a new project with the term nearly at an end. So they concentrated on stripping canvases for the year-end exhibit, which engendered a lot of horseplay, which Jay was too distracted to deal with. Firmness had never been her long suit.

By the time she got home, it was threatening to rain. In spite of all the thunder, it had held off the night before. But now the thunder rumbled almost constantly. The warm humid air was heavy with the fragrance of a zillion blossoms. Spring was her favorite of all the seasons, despite the fact that it clogged her sinuses and sapped her energy. What she'd like better than anything else in the world was to lie under a weeping willow, on a certain creek bank in Wilkes County, and daydream.

Jay had always been good at daydreaming. One of the things that had gotten her into trouble as a child had been a tendency to daydream when she should have been doing something more productive.

Such as cleaning out a potting shed that had become a repository for all those things that were too old to be useful, but too good to throw away, she told herself. That was certainly productive enough. Not to mention hot. Even in shorts and a halter, she was sweating. Glowing, as Great-Aunt Ruth would have put it. Ladies didn't sweat.

On her way home from school, she'd stopped by the market and collected several empty boxes, which wouldn't begin to hold all the used clay pots and empty canning jars, but it was a start. Tomorrow she would make a run to the dump, which was actually more of a social event than a chore, since she usually ran into at least one person she knew there, and ended up visiting and, as often as not, swapping junk.

She had filled up four boxes and was beginning to visualize the ten-by-ten room all clean and scrubbed, with the three tall windows uncluttered and washed, when she became aware of an odd sound. Sort of an aggressive . . . hissing?

Carefully, she began to back out. She hadn't grown up on a farm without discovering that snakes sometimes denned up in old outbuildings. Did copperheads hiss? Or buzz?

She was nearly out the door when she felt the first sting. Halfway down the steps, another one struck her on the right cheek, just under the eye, and then they were everywhere, so thick she could actually smell them.

Bees!

Waving her arms over her head, she ran toward the house, and felt three more stings on her back before she reached the side door. Her eye was beginning to feel odd. She wasn't allergic—not dangerously allergic, anyway, but she swelled and hurt, and unless she got the stingers out, she would itch for days.

Without even pausing to think, she dashed through the side door, up the back stairs and ran down the second-floor hall to the room Thad used as a study. "Oh, help, I need you!" she cried, bursting through the door.

The man who swung around to confront her was a stranger. Wearing a pair of hip-hugging jeans, he was bare-chested, barefooted and barefaced. And there was nothing the least bit baggy about him!

She hung in the doorway, staring, her hair stuck to her damp face, one eye rapidly swelling shut, her paint-stained shorts and halter damp and clinging to her body. "Professor? Th-Thad?"

He stared right back. "What the devil happened to your face?"

The frozen tableau lasted only a few seconds. And then he was beside her, and the eyes that had looked dark and dangerous for one brief moment were back to thoughtful and gentle. His hands, as he drew her into the room, were gentle, too, and Jay began to tremble.

"Aftershock," she gasped. "Bees. D-Daddy always said they swarmed in thundery weather, I just f-f-forgot. N-n-nothing serious, but it hurts like blazes."

He took her face between his hands and tilted it toward the pale light spilling in through the open window, and she noticed that his hair, wet and several shades darker than usual, was dripping down his muscular neck. "You won't be able to see out of this if we don't stop the swelling," he murmured.

For an instant she was so shocked by the effect of his nearness, his touch, that she almost forgot her bee stings. Her nostrils were assailed by the scent of healthy male skin, fresh from the shower. The animal warmth radiating out from his lean, hard flesh seemed to envelop her in a safe cocoon, and she drew in a deep, shuddering breath, which only made matters worse.

Merciful heavens, she was losing it. "I—I can take care of it—I don't know why I panicked, I never panic." She was babbling, trembling and hurting like the very devil, and all she could do was stare at the snap on his jeans, which was undone, as if he'd only just pulled up his zipper and hadn't had time to finish dressing.

"Shh, be still. I've got a field kit around here somewhere."

By the time the professor finished applying first aid to all her stings, Jay had got a grip on herself. She was breathing normally, and able to think in more-or-less coherent segments.

"I'd better—no, I suppose it's too late, but—is that rain? Oh, my banana boxes will melt! I couldn't find a single seafood box."

"A cool pack on that eye might help. I think the other places will be okay. Could I help with your, uh—banana boxes?"

Her shoulders sagged. It had been a long day, and she had yet to accomplish a single thing she'd set out to do. "Thanks, but it's only flowerpots," she said, and turning to leave, missed his look of baffled amusement.

He stopped her at the door with a hand on her arm. "Jay—are you sure you're all right? Not feeling dizzy or anything like that? Some people have, uh—reactions to bee venom.''

"I've already had all the reaction I'm going to have. I always hurt like the devil, swell up a little, itch a little and that's it. Really, it's no big deal, but thanks for being here. I could never have reached the places on my back to pull the stingers out."

Her gaze strayed over his rugged, irregular features. No one in their right mind could call him handsome—not like Mike Weems. Or even Bob Haverty. So why was it that a kiss from Mike was about as exciting as stale popcorn, while a single touch from Thad Blanchard sizzled all the way down to her toes, blowing out every circuit along the way?

Electricity in the atmosphere, she rationalized. That and the bee venom swimming through her system. Really, it was no big deal, she thought, smiling in a way that had Thad staring at the empty doorway long moments after she'd gone, wondering what was so special about a pair of big, gray-green eyes, a few freckles and a chipped incisor?

Something didn't add up, he told himself as he finished dressing, collected the bundle of khakis and white shirts and headed for the launderette.

5

━━━◆◆━━━

By the time Jay got home from a trip to the grocery store, rain was drumming against the roof of her car, flooding the gutters, turning the landscape into an Impressionistic blur of pastel colors. Leaves stuck to the windshield for a moment before being sent on their way by a swash of the wiper blade.

There'd be no more work done in the potting shed today. A trip to the dump was out of the question. With her painting time being rapidly gobbled up with unproductive exercises, she was fighting the urge to call and cancel her exhibit.

But if she gave in this time, the next time it would be easier to quit, and the next time easier still. She had never taken the coward's way out before; she refused to do it now. Somehow, she would paint the damned show, if it killed her.

The bottom fell out just as she pulled into the driveway. Resigned to waiting for the rain to slack off, she shut off the engine, leaned her head back and and closed her eyes.

She was still waiting a few minutes later when the passenger side door was wrenched open and Thad Blanchard squeezed in beside her.

Rain soaked, Thad grinned at her. "Saw you drive up, thought you might need an umbrella."

"What on earth were you doing outside in this flood?"

He didn't answer right away, and when he mentioned something about rolling up the windows of his own car, she had the strangest feeling he had just snatched an excuse out of the air.

Wind-stripped leaves plastered the steamy windows. As the rain continued to drum down, obscuring the world outside the cramped confines, the intimacy grew. After one penetrating glance, Thad turned and stared straight ahead. Jay toyed with her keys.

"So where's the umbrella?" she asked finally.

"Umbrella? Oh. Yeah. Wind caught it and turned it inside out. It's under the porte cochere."

She wondered why he'd bothered to come out at all, in that case.

She wondered why the faint scent of plastic rain gear, soap and wet male skin should affect her so much more than Mike's expensive cologne.

She wondered what had happened to her resolution not to get involved with the strangers she was forced to share her house with. Maybe leasing out her second floor had been a mistake after all, yet she desperately needed every penny she could earn if she was going to hang on to her home.

In Jay's family, home was the center of the universe. The home she had grown up in had been built by her grandparents. When her father had stopped farming his acreage, he had divided the land up among his children. Jay's older brother had built a home on his portion. Jay had gone off to college, met Ronnie Turner in her junior year, married him in her senior year, and by that time, a few rocky acres of Wilkes County farmland had ceased to seem so important. It had been at Ronnie's urging soon after they'd married that she had sold her seven acres and put the entire amount into a down payment on the twelve-room fixer-upper on the outskirts of Chapel Hill that was not only to be their home, but was going to become a bonanza once they'd turned it into a bed and breakfast.

By the time Ronnie had died, Jay had long since given up on the bed-and-breakfast notion, having found out in the meantime all the expense and red tape that entailed. Still, she'd been desperate to hang on to the house, if only because the equity it represented was all she had left of the heritage she'd been so quick to squander.

Her salary as an art teacher was enough to live on—barely. Her painting habit supported itself—barely. Renting out her second floor to staff or faculty from the university—quiet, responsible people who would mind their own business and not interfere with hers—

had seemed like a good idea at the time, and except for a few minor incidents, it had worked well. All she asked of her tenants was that they pay in advance and not intrude in her life any more than necessary.

Surely that was not too much to ask?

Even with the sound of the rain beating down all around them, the silence seemed profound. When she could stand it no more, she clenched her keys in her fist and said, "It's beginning to slack off. I'm going to make a run for it."

"Let me give you my raincoat." Thad leaned to one side, worked his left arm out of a sleeve and managed to jab her on the shoulder in the process. Mumbling apologies, he struggled with the other sleeve, cracked his forearm on the dashboard and swore under his breath.

"No, please—I won't get wet if I run now. Look, it's almost stopped."

It hadn't, but if she stayed shut up with him a moment longer, breathing in his scent, feeling his heat—unable to keep from stealing glances at his thighs, every muscle clearly defined in those clinging wet khakis, she wouldn't be responsible for her own actions.

The trouble was, since the business with the bee stings, she could no longer look at the man without picturing him fresh from the shower in unsnapped jeans—barefooted, bare-chested, his face uncluttered by anything more than the shadow of stubble on his jaw.

Without waiting for him to finish removing his coat, she opened her door, ducked her head and ran for the house. By the time she reached the front porch she was soaked to the skin, but soaking was better than being shut up in a small car with a man like Thaddeus Blanchard.

Jay tried to tell herself it was just because he was so big. That he took up too much space.

The trouble was, the man was entirely too distracting, and the last thing she needed at this point in her life was one more distraction.

Tomorrow night she had a date with the girls, she reminded herself as she stepped out of her shoes on the front porch and shook off her skirt. The next night she'd promised to go to a concert, which was probably a good thing. If she spent a little more time in the company of men like Mike Weems, she might spend less time daydreaming about men like her professor.

At this rate, by the time she got back to her easel again, she would have forgotten how to paint. Through absolutely no fault of her own, her neat, orderly life was disintegrating all around her.

More than an hour later, when Thad rapped politely on her studio door to ask if she wanted him to pick up her supper when he picked up his own, Jay declined. Busy packing up boxes of art supplies to be moved as soon as the shed was ready, she thanked him politely and closed the door.

A little guiltily, she told herself she could have offered to make him an omelet when she made her own, but that might have established a dangerous precedent.

Another dangerous precedent.

Guilt. Everyone had warned her against getting involved in the personal lives of the people who leased her second floor. She couldn't agree more. Now that she had her own life arranged the way she wanted it, she intended to see that it stayed that way. It had taken her years to recover from Ronnie's death. His debts, his tangled finances, dealing with his personal belongings—those had been bad enough, but the guilt she'd felt because her grief hadn't been totally devastating had been hardest to deal with.

So she stacked another box on the ones beside the door and went into the kitchen and fried a single strip of bacon to go with her cottage-cheese-and-tomato omelet, telling herself that, after all, she wasn't running a boardinghouse.

But a little while later, eating her solitary meal from a willowware plate on a cheerful blue-and-white checked tablecloth spread over her maple kitchen table, she pictured the professor all alone upstairs, eating something cold and greasy from a plastic tray.

A man needed—

No, darn it, she refused to fall into that trap! Men were every bit as capable as women were of feeding themselves. Even Ronnie had been a passable cook. So he'd been a perennial undergraduate. So even after he'd more or less dropped out of school, he hadn't been able to hold down a job more than a few months at a time. The professor was obviously cut from a different bolt of cloth.

Of course, everything had been different in her parents' day. Back in those days, men didn't drop dead at the age of thirty-one while jogging down Rosemary Street in a pair of two-hundred-dollar shoes and a cerulean blue silk running suit with neon orange racing stripes.

Back in her parents' day, women were expected to stay home and look after their families while men went out and slogged in the salt mines to earn a living. It was far from a perfect plan, but at least all the players knew their roles and everything usually worked out reasonably well in the end.

Back in those days of innocence, how many young unmarried women owned their own homes and lived their own independent lives, answerable only to God and Caesar?

"So, what's your point, Turner?" Jay grumbled as she rose to scrape out the last of her omelet.

Tuesday, between school and her birthday dinner date, Jay loaded the trunk and back seat of her car with several cartons of clay pots and canning jars that had found a home in the potting shed. Thad must have set the boxes back inside before the rain began, along with a stack of wonderful waxed seafood cartons he had evidently scrounged from the market.

"Bless you," she said softly, estimating the space on the wall shelves and frowning at a damp section of flooring where the roof had been leaking. Given a choice, she'd much rather have stayed home and gotten on with the cleaning, moving and resettling so that she could get back to painting before her fickle muse deserted her altogether.

But birthdays were a tradition, and traditions were to be valued, and good friends were to be valued most of all. Once the school term ended, she could make up for lost time.

They argued over the movie menu, then decided on an early dinner and shopping at the mall instead. Sue and Sara headed for the lingerie department, C.A. for housewares, while Jay browsed in the arts-and-crafts shop. Then they all met at an appointed time and place for dessert and coffee. They had always shopped independently, then joined forces.

All three women had bought her silly frippery birthday gifts. "But you've already given me my birthday gift," Jay protested, laughing as she dipped into her Double Hysterical Chocolate Delight.

"Why do I get the idea you didn't appreciate it?" Sue teased.

"Actually, it wasn't all bad," Jay admitted. A subliminal flash of Thad waiting on the porch swing, of Thad kneeling in the foyer, one leg angled out stiffly at one side while he helped her gather up her things, flashed through her mind, and she blinked it away.

"I'm seeing the Sunday guy again on Wednesday night."

"Mike Weems, right?" Sue counted off on her fingers. "Flunked out of dental school, divorced, taking a business course. Five-eleven, dark curly hair, blue eyes, wears a Rolex, subleased an apartment out on Jones Ferry Road."

Jay's mouth fell open. *Flunked out of dental school?*

Men and their prickly little egos. Ronnie had never been able to admit to failure, either.

"Suzanne, how on earth do you know all that?" C.A. marveled.

"Friends in high places."

"High, my foot! You mean friends in nosy places."

"Does he wear anything besides a wristwatch?" Sara wanted to know.

"Mephisto, Brooks Brothers—"

"Sue, stop that." Jay tried hard to sound outraged and not amused.

"What, before I even find out what color his jockeys are? Give me a day or two and I'll check with my sources. Of course, by that time, you'll probably have found out for yourself if what I've heard about him is true."

"What? What have you heard? If what's true?"

"That he likes older women. My sources say he's dated a few since he moved in, and that they all looked older than he does, but hey! Maybe they're just doing his laundry or something, right? The maternal thing?"

"Remember that song that came out a few years ago? Something about older women making better lovers?"

"*Some* older women, maybe. Others substitute chocolate and geriatric vitamins." Sue cut her eyes at Jay, and they all giggled.

Giggled all the way to the parking lot. Even when she unlocked her front door and slipped inside the house, balancing a purse and three exceedingly tacky birthday gifts, Jay was still smiling.

It had been a wonderful evening. Good friends were priceless, even when they insisted on poking their collective noses into her business and giving her fake fingernails with the signs of the zodiac on them, and a musical toilet paper roller and a T-shirt with an extremely suggestive slogan about artists and how they did it.

Upstairs, a door opened. Only then did Jay allow herself to admit she'd been half expecting him to wait up for her—would have been disappointed if he hadn't.

"Have a good time?" Thad called down softly.

"Wonderful. By the way, thanks for dragging my junk in out of the rain—and for all those empty seafood cartons."

"Sure."

She waited for him to come downstairs. When he didn't, she smiled uncertainly and said, "Well... thanks again. And good night."

* * *

Thad made it back to the bedroom and groaned softly as he eased his weight down. Most of the scars from his recent encounter with unfriendly fire had faded, but in damp weather he still caught hell from the bullet that had grazed his femur. It hadn't helped that he'd whacked his thigh on a damned birdbath while trying to raise a ladder so that he could cut off a limb that had fallen on one of the gutters.

He had about as much business trying to play house as a warthog had playing tennis. Not for the first time, he wondered why he hadn't simply rented a room in a motel for the duration. So it would've been noisier and probably costlier. At least he'd have had maid service and there'd be no risk of getting involved with his neighbors.

No risk of getting any stupid ideas about hearths and homes, either—or the women who made them into something more than just a collection of sticks and stones. As a dues-paying member of the so-called boomer generation, he should have known better.

He'd had another letter from Cyn today. His ex-wife. That was three this week alone. Cyn had a tendency to get maudlin when she was on the bottle—which happened when she was between men. Which happened more and more often these days. She'd been nineteen when they'd married seventeen years ago. Twenty when she'd walked out on him. Which meant she was thirty-six now. Old enough to know better.

He'd paid for rehabilitation a few times before he'd found out that instead of drying out, she'd used the last money he'd sent her for a fling in the Bahamas. After that, he'd refused, but she still wrote when she was down, and his mail drop forwarded her letters. He seemed to represent some sort of security in her messy life, God knows why. He didn't even represent security in his own life.

Lying on his back, Thad stared up at the high ceiling, at the ornate crown molding. His gaze strayed to the green tiled fireplace that had been sealed off with a cast-iron panel picturing a kid, a few bushes and a bunch of black sheep.

What kind of man would build a house like this? A house that was meant to stand against time, giving not only physical shelter, but emotional sustenance to generations of sons and grandsons?

What kind of woman would stand beside such a man through war and pestilence, through the good times and bad, raising his children, drilling into them all those hackneyed old platitudes about thrift and hard work, honor and Mom's apple pie?

Basic human nature hadn't changed all that much. But something had sure as hell changed. Somewhere along the way, something had broken down.

More and more often as he grew older, holding in his hand a relic from another age, Thad wondered about it. Which was, he supposed, a perfectly natural occupational hazard for an anthropologist. Wondering about people and the way they lived their lives.

Wondering what was important to them—what their goals had been. How they'd reacted when those goals had been met. Or had fallen apart in their hands.

All of which probably explained why he'd spent so much time thinking about his landlady, he told himself. Habit. The old occupational syndrome.

He jeered silently. Sure it was. It was strictly an exercise in intellectual curiosity, wondering what kind of perfume she wore and where she put it on her body—wondering what she wore to bed, or if she wore anything at all. Wondering what she would be like in bed. Shy? Demanding? Bored?

Wondering if she'd come apart in his arms and then lie there afterward, savoring a special feeling of closeness—one that should have been the most intimate feeling in the world, but somehow never was.

At least, not in his experience. Women, in his experience, wanted to talk or they wanted more sex, or they wanted to go repair their makeup, or they wanted a drink and a cigarette. Some of them wanted to watch TV. Some didn't even bother to turn the TV off before climbing into bed. Some wanted money. Some wanted special favors.

Jeez! Talk about a case of arrested development! Forty-one years old, three degrees and half a dozen articles published in respectable journals, and here he was, bogged down in a pathetic, adolescent wet dream that had about as much basis in reality as a holographic image. Less, in fact.

What he needed was a cold shower.

What he *really* needed was to get an outline of his book down on paper before the term began, break his PC out of storage and pray the damned wiring in this old tomb wouldn't let him down.

When Jay got in on Wednesday afternoon, the message light on her answering machine was blinking rapidly. Leaving her gear on the hall table along with the mail, which she hadn't even taken time to sort, she dashed up the eight steps and punched the Play button. Turpentine and too many interruptions from the telephone might add up to a loophole in the lease Thad had signed. And she was getting used to having the professor around.

It was Sam from the bookstore. A poetry reading he thought she probably wouldn't be interested in.

Wouldn't?

"But even if you are, you'll probably be too busy," the tape continued.

"Great snakes alive, man, get a backbone!" she muttered.

Sam's timorous voice went on to say that if by any chance she was interested, he would be glad to pick her up at seven-fifteen, and afterward, maybe they could go out to this new restaurant that had just opened up that served great barbecue, or anyplace else she'd rather go, but she probably wasn't interested, he just thought he'd ask.

Jay swore a ladylike oath and stared at the flat black box as the tape whirred itself back to the beginning.

"Trouble?"

She looked up to see her stealthy tenant at the head of the stairs. "Oh, hi. No, not really trouble—at least, I'm pretty sure it wasn't intended that way, but—"

"But you feel guilty because he's such a pathetic case, right?"

Immediately her defensive hackles rose, ready to deny the charge, but then she laughed. "You're right. Not that it makes sense."

"So what are you going to do?"

She shrugged, suddenly tired from the collapse of her orderly regime. Discipline always fell apart near the end of a term. "What do you think I should do?"

Thad's eyebrows, those devilish slanted wings, twitched. He took off his glasses and polished them on his shirttail. "Me? I'd tell him to grow up," he said.

"No, you wouldn't. You're far too kind. You'd probably do exactly what I'm going to do, which is wait a day or so and then call him back when I can think of a really, really good excuse—one that won't crush his fragile ego."

Thad slipped his glasses on again—the Jekyll–Hyde thing—and chuckled. "I hate to disillusion you, Ms. Turner, but there's not a kind bone in my body. Believe me, I know. Bones are my specialty."

Shoulders sagging, she turned to go downstairs. At the moment, reminding him of the several small acts of kindness he had shown in just the few weeks he'd been living under her roof took more energy than she possessed.

Thad watched her go. He couldn't figure her out. Not that he professed to be any great expert on women—at least not in the living flesh. JeanAnn Turner struck him as an odd blend of traits. She certainly qualified as a feminist. Self-supporting, independent, a career woman who owned her own home and managed her own life with every evidence of success.

But that wasn't the sum total of Ms. Turner. No way. Something about the lady was out of focus. Sometimes he felt as if he were looking through two negatives superimposed, trying to separate two tantalizing women from two different generations.

He put it down to one more occupational hazard, brought on by too many years spent extrapolating ancient life-styles from a few fibers, a few fragments of bone, a bit of carbon and a handful of potsherds.

Absently, he plugged in his coffeemaker and retrieved a bottle of cognac from between two stacks of books. He took time to change out of the white oxford-cloth shirt into an identical shirt from the stack he'd brought back from the launderette, clean, folded but unironed.

And then he went downstairs, armed with a coffeepot, a bottle, and two mugs, whistling an extremely bawdy song he'd picked up from a seaman on a freighter working out of a Baltic seaport.

She was in her studio, still wearing the dress she'd worn to school. Her hair, which he happened to know usually started out the day in a neat bundle at the back of her head, was trailing untidily over her shoulder.

It looked sexy as hell.

"I thought you could use a boost. Cognac and caffeine?"

"I shouldn't," she demurred, but he could see by the way her eyes lit up, by the flush of color in her pale cheeks that didn't quite obliterate the light sprinkling of freckles, that she was tempted.

Why was it that women with freckles had such velvety skin? It had to be genetic, yet he'd never before given it any thought.

He poured while she cleared off another chair. There were two in the room, both straight chairs, both paint stained.

"Here we go... Dr. Blanchard's patented remedy," he said, filling both mugs and topping them off with the brandy. "Guaranteed to lift sagging spirits, cure ingrown toenails and assuage the pangs of a guilty conscience."

Jay began to laugh. She took a sip, shuddered at the bite and then laughed some more—laughed until tears overflowed her eyes, and Thad gently removed the mug from her hand, knelt in front of her chair and toppled her over onto his shoulder. His leg was killing him, but God, he had never known such a sweet armful of woman in his entire life. Some things were worth hurting for.

6

"This is silly. I never cry," Jay wept. "Honestly, I'm not crying, I just can't seem to stop laughing, and—" She sniffed, lifted herself from his arms and knuckled her red-rimmed eyes. "It must be the weather. I'm allergic to pollen. Or the brandy."

"Right. Nothing at all to do with the fact that you leave the house at the crack of dawn, come home limp as a shoestring, grab a rake or a mop or a broom or a paintbrush and—"

"That's not true," Jay protested.

"What's not true? That you're burning the candle at both ends?"

"I'd hardly call it candle burning—one concert, one movie, an outdoor exhibit and a reading at a bookstore. You make it sound as if I'm on the go all the time."

His glasses slid down half a notch. One winged eyebrow lifted as he regarded her skeptically, and Jay gulped down half her enriched coffee and shuddered. She had eased off her cork-soled canvas flats, and now she studied her ankles, raised her toes and watched her metatarsals come into play as if they were the most fascinating gadgets on earth.

A residual hiccup escaped her, and without comment Thad handed her a large white handkerchief. She took it and mopped her eyes. It smelled of laundry soap. *He* smelled of laundry soap. And some faintly spicy toilet soap. And occasionally, of cigar smoke, which reminded her of her father, which was probably the reason her emotions got all out of kilter when she was around him for any length of time.

"Maybe I'm just homesick," she said with an apologetic smile.

"You? I thought this was your home."

Which was how she found herself telling him all about the plans she and Ronnie had once had for the house, and how Ronnie had died, and she'd been forced to reel in her dreams. She talked about her job as an art teacher, and the criticism she drew from her peers because she refused to arbitrarily change her style of painting in order to keep up with the times.

"Even if I could do it, it would feel dishonest—contrived. Eventually I might evolve into something a little less traditional, but by then everyone else will have moved even farther out. A few years ago, someone dumped a load of old plumbing pipes at the landfill. I thought about gluing them together and entering them in a sculpture show."

Thad grinned and refilled their mugs.

"Well, who could say it wasn't art? When I was a freshman in college some visiting artist had a truckload of construction rubble dumped into a room at a local gallery. Right through the window. He stuck a flag on top, called it Eden Revisited and won a prize for it."

"So why not go him one better and enter the whole landfill where it stands? I'm not sure where you'd sign your name—maybe you could find a discarded mailbox in the heap."

"Spoken like a learned critic."

"One man's art, as the saying goes. I'd like to show you my favorite kind of art someday."

"I'd like to see it."

"Unfortunately, it's an out-of-town exhibit. Cave paintings. Ancient weavings. Records carved in stone by people who lived and loved and fought and died thousands of years ago."

He fell silent, and so did she, wondering how she could ever have thought him dull and unimaginative.

Had she thought him dull and unimaginative?

Not really. She simply hadn't thought of him at all. Probably because he was as nondescript and as comfortable to be around as an old shoe.

Not!

She grinned, hearing the echo of last year's favorite classroom catchword. Seeing him now, his chair tilted back against the wall, his feet propped against a bundle of canvas stretchers and his arms crossed over his chest, Jay wondered idly how he stayed in such great physical condition. She'd never seen any indi-

cation that he ran or worked out or did anything of
that nature.

And because she felt uncomfortable thinking of him
that way—physically—she began to talk about the
farm, about Great-Aunt Ruth who, at eighty-one, still
won blue ribbons for her pickled okra, and her sister
Ava, who was a meteorologist in Kodiak, and her
other sister, Helen, who had two sets of twins, and her
brother, Leonard, Jr., who had once raced a '63 Chevy
from Wilkesboro to Sparta on pure grain alcohol
supplied by a cousin who had explained to the reve-
nuers that what he manufactured out behind his silo
was high-octane fuel, and he was shocked to think
they would accuse him of making moonshine!

"You've got to be making that up."

"You don't know Len and Cousin Tiny. They managed to get me into trouble every day of my life until I
went off to college."

Chuckling, Thad refilled their cups, and Jay waited
for him to tell her about his family.

And waited.

Finally, emboldened by the brandy, she blurted,
"Do you have any brothers or sisters?" Or a wife or a
child, she wanted to ask, but didn't.

"Not that I know of," he replied, which she thought
was a rather strange way of putting it.

"You're from somewhere up north?"

He nodded. "I hope you're not moving your painting gear outdoors on my account," he said. "I don't
mind the smell of turpentine."

Jay's shoulders sagged. "*Now* you tell me," she groaned.

"You're actually going to all this trouble on account of a few casual remarks I might have made?"

"Might have made? Did I just imagine you complaining about the whole house reeking like a—what was it you called it? A naval stores depot?"

And then he found himself explaining the historical importance of naval stores, which she, as a Tarheel, should have known. Which led to an explanation of how he came to be familiar with various seaports around the world, which led to explaining the kind of things an anthropologist sometimes had crated and shipped from one country to another, or one museum to another.

All of which Jay found fascinating, only it didn't answer a single one of the more personal questions bursting to be asked. Her eyes took on a dreamy expression as she leaned forward, hooked her bare heels on a chair rung and braced her elbows on her knees. Propping her chin in her hands, she allowed herself to fall deeper and deeper under the spell of that quiet, vibrant male voice.

He was a compelling lecturer. Jay found herself envying his students as he sketched in word pictures so skillfully that she could actually feel the dry heat, smell the dust and the pungent herbs that grew wild on exotic foreign hillsides, hear the babble of half a dozen dialects, the creak of heavy ropes and the braying of asses.

With words alone, he transmitted the infectious thrill of discovering an ancient hearth that had last been used thousands of years ago.

Or held in his hand the bones of an extinct animal that had fallen to a hunter armed with no more than a fire-hardened stick.

Or uncovered the skeletal remains of a woman who had crossed the Bering Straits on foot, suffering from arthritis and borderline malnutrition, borne at least one child, broken her leg in a fall and died where she lay. Probably from exposure.

"If you can tell so much by only a few bones, how much can you tell from a real live person?" She was beginning to feel uncomfortably exposed. Those scratched eyeglass lenses hid a pair of eyes that saw far too much.

"More. And less."

"That's no answer." But she wasn't sure she wanted to know the answer. Sipping her cooling coffee, she was reluctant to leave, even knowing it was growing late. The warm glow that had spread through her body was entirely too pleasurable. She was no longer tired. She was no longer even tense. In fact, she couldn't remember when she'd felt more relaxed.... Which was strange, because they were practically strangers and she was never at ease with strangers.

Thad grinned. He folded his glasses and slid them into his shirt pocket. They were bifocals, the tops clear glass. He'd long since discovered that the only way to have them on hand when he needed to see something at close range was to wear them all the time.

He knew what he'd *like* to see at close range. A lot closer than the half-dozen feet that separated their two chairs. Even from here, though, he could see every freckle on her velvety skin, which included several dozen across her nose and cheeks, fewer on her brow and chin—none at all on her throat. Her long, supple, graceful throat.

He shifted in his chair and slung one leg up across his other knee. *If you're going to think about her, man, think bones, not flesh!*

He thought bones, but it didn't help. His gaze strayed down her long, slender legs to her ankles and her elegant feet. He liked a woman with elegant feet. Not that he had a foot fetish or anything, and not that he had anything against short, square feet. Or chubby ones. Or, hell, hairy ones with hooves or claws, for that matter—only, hers just happened to be unusually attractive.

He thought about her hands. The same long, elegant bones—a few paint stains around the nails. A few calluses. He liked the fluttery way she used them to make a point when she was talking. It made him wonder what they would feel like fluttering over his naked body. Making a point.

Making him wild!

"What time is your date picking you up?" he asked in an effort to break up a thought pattern that could only lead to trouble.

You'd have thought he'd yelled "Fire!"

She jumped up, slapped a hand to her brow and swayed on her elegant naked feet, and he was fool enough to take advantage of her momentary dizziness.

"Whoa, there—you stood up too fast," he said, catching her in his arms. If he hadn't held her close, he told himself, she might have fallen and hurt herself. So he held her close enough to smell the rainy-flower-garden scent that always seemed to cling to her skin.

"It's the brandy," she gasped. "I'm not used to it."

But she didn't pull away, and Thad was stunned by the powerful need that came over him to sweep her up into his arms and carry her to his bed and keep her there all night—all week—until he was forced to go out and forage for food.

Talk about your primitive urges!

Gradually, Jay realized that she had wrapped her arms around him, and that he was hard as sun-warmed granite. Blinking, she focused on his eyes, which were dark brown with flecks of gold. Beautiful eyes. Eyes that were unusually intense.

Eyes that were entirely too close!

Feeling like a rabbit in a snare, she flung her arms free and shoved against his chest. Then, like a royal klutz, she stepped back onto one of her discarded shoes and staggered again.

"Better let me help you," Thad said gruffly.

"No thanks! It was your help that got me in this condition in the first place. Your brandy, I mean." Or his deep, compelling voice. Or those wicked eyes... "I'd better—you'd better— Oh, Lordy, I'm going to be late!" She glanced at her watch, scooped up her shoes and waited pointedly for him to leave.

Which he did, heading for the front stairs, and then she wanted to call him back. She wished while he'd been asking her all those questions about her work and her family, she had asked a few herself.

She had. Only, he hadn't bothered to answer. Which was probably just as well, because the last thing she needed was to get herself all tangled up in the affairs of a tenant who was only here for a single term. Maybe two, but nothing more permanent. She leased on a three- or a six-month basis. He'd taken the three.

Funny, she thought idly as she showered and got dressed for her date. If ever a man felt permanent, it was Thaddeus Blanchard. Permanent as rock. Permanent as the petrified bones he was so fond of. Gentle, thoughtful, warm, solid, sexy—

Good Lord, where had *that* thought come from?

The music was depressing, but Mike looked like Hollywood incarnate in white slacks and a mauve silk shirt. The color made his skin look like it sported a golden tan, and he was masculine enough to carry it off. He was also wearing a pendant and an earring, and on him they looked terrific. As an artist, Jay appreciated well-designed jewelry. During her college years she had taken two courses in jewelry design and made several nice pieces in silver. Which were now gathering tarnish in the top drawer of her dresser. Ronnie had preferred gold.

Idly, she tried and failed to picture Thad wearing a baroque pendant and a single gold stud.

Someone in the small audience coughed. Hauling in her wandering attention, Jay laced her fingers together and pinned an interested look on her face as the chamber group launched into what surely must be their last number. They'd been playing for what seemed hours, and one of the wires in her underwire bra was digging into her rib cage.

Mike leaned closer, favoring her with a whiff of cologne and toothpaste. "What's your tolerance for chamber music, JayJay?"

"Not as great as I thought," she whispered back.

"How do you stand on Ravel?"

"Carefully. Very, very carefully. I tried painting to the *Bolero* once, but it's a little too—too compulsive. Actually, what I really like is—"

"Shh!"

Jay grimaced at the chorus of shushes from nearby seats, and winking, Mike rose and held out his hand. The two of them scurried like guilty children from the auditorium.

"Sorry about the bill of fare. I was expecting something on the lighter side."

"I know about lite beer and lite salad dressing, but lite *chamber music?*"

With a grin that alone could have won him a screen test, Mike held open the door and they emerged into the warm, fragrant night. "Okay, I confess. Actually, I was trying to impress you with my musical erudition," he confided, which she found rather touching. To her knowledge, no one had ever deliberately tried to impress her. "When it comes to music, I'm really into jazz, but I had you figured for the highbrow stuff."

He was still holding her hand. Jay saw no need to make an issue of it. Sodium vapor lights cast a friendly pink glow over the wet pavement. There'd evidently been another shower while they were inside.

And then he swung around in front of her, a look of boyish delight on his face. "Hey—I just had a great idea! There's a first-rate sound system in my apartment, so why don't we stop by somewhere and pick up a couple of CDs and go home and listen. We each get to pick one, my treat."

CDs? She'd been expecting perhaps an offer of drinks, or ice cream, or maybe even a late supper. "You mean—actually go out and buy records? CDs?" Jay was still playing her old LPs, much to the disgust of Sue and Sara, who told her vinyl was extinct. C.A. was the only one who seemed to understand that if she switched to CDs, her entire lifetime collection of opera albums would become obsolete.

Besides, a CD player wasn't in her budget.

Mike slung an arm around her waist as they crossed the parking lot. "Sure, why not? I promised you an evening of music, and hey, I'm a man of my word!"

They spent almost an hour in the record shop. Jay tried to choose something they could both enjoy, since Mike would be stuck with it, but he liked jazz and jazz gave her a stomachache. It always sounded as if each musician was playing from a different score.

There was an album with a desert scene on the cover that reminded her of one of the stories Thad had told earlier. She wondered what kind of music he enjoyed. Or if he even enjoyed music. All she'd ever heard from upstairs was news programs, usually foreign.

Did he dance?

Slow dancing—that would be his style. Hers, too. Dancing was another one of those high-tech things that kept changing before she could get the hang of it—at least the way her students did it. She'd never been enough of an exhibitionist to feel comfortable on the dance floor.

"You say you like Ravel?" Mike held up his choice. "There was this movie a few years ago..."

Actually, she hadn't said she liked Ravel, but if he did, then she could go along with it.

They ended up with Relativity, which was an Irish group that had played frequently in the area, and the Ravel, which he insisted she would love, and headed west toward Jones Ferry Road, driving a little too fast for her comfort.

There wasn't much traffic. It was probably that—that and the speed—that caused her to entertain a few second thoughts. It was past her bedtime and she was on her way to visit a strange man in his own apartment. What did she know about him, other than the fact that he claimed to be a dentist, he wore expensive shoes, expensive jewelry and pastel colors? He drove a red sports car that must have cost more than her annual salary, and he was almost too handsome, which made her wonder, not for the first time, what he was doing answering a personals ad in the first place. All he would have to do was crook his little finger to have women crawling out of the woodwork.

Mike was whistling tunelessly under his breath—jazz, no doubt—when suddenly he slammed on his brakes. In spite of her shoulder belt, which she'd loosened because shoulder belts always slid up over her breasts and threatened to strangle her, Jay was flung forward.

Before she could catch her breath, Mike had swerved over to the side of the street and switched off the engine. With a single crude oath, he leapt out of the car and ran around to the front of the hood.

Jay's breath came in shallow little gasps. She felt clammy, but she wasn't actually hurt. At least she didn't think she was. Her belt hadn't been all that loose. But she was badly shaken, and when Mike slid in beside her, muttering about dogs and insurance and using a few words that not even her toughest student had ever used in her presence, she pulled herself together.

"What happened?"

"A damned dog. The son of a bitch broke my grill!"

"Is he hurt? Oh, Lord yes—he would be. Maybe we can get him to a vet in time—do you have anything in your trunk to wrap—"

"For God's sake, woman, if you think I'm going to waste my time on any mangy mutt that cost me five hundred bucks, you're crazy!"

Nausea churned suddenly in her stomach. "Five hundred dollars?"

"Deductible! I've got five hundred dollar deductible! That flea-bitten scumbag wasted my grill! I'll be lucky if the whole front end doesn't have to be replaced!"

"Is he...dead?"

"I hope to God he is, because if he's not, he damned well soon will be!"

She closed her eyes, sick at the way the evening had turned out. Sick over the way Mike had turned out. Sick about the poor dog, who had done nothing more than try to cross the street.

"I have to see," she said quietly. She unclipped her belt and opened her door.

"Jay! Dammit, get back in here!"

The dog was definitely dead. With his neck twisted in that unnatural way, he couldn't be anything else. Unaware of the tears running down her cheeks, Jay grabbed hold of his back legs and tugged him off to one side, out of the way of traffic. "I'm sorry," she whispered, wondering if he had a name, if he belonged to a child, or if he was just a stray, which, in a way, was even sadder. She'd have been glad to give him a home. "I'm so sorry," she whispered again.

Mike stared straight ahead, not acknowledging her by so much as a look when she let herself back into the car. She felt for her purse in the floor and took out a wad of tissues. The smell of dirty wet dog seemed to permeate the air.

She didn't care; no dog deserved to die like that.

"Are you quite through?" Mike asked, and she could tell his teeth were clenched.

"Yes. Thank you. If you turn right at the next corner and go a block and take another right, it's a straight shot to my street."

He leaned his head back, closed his eyes and sighed heavily. "It's been a bust all around, hasn't it? Look, for what it's worth, I'm sorry, JayJay. I guess we'd better call it a night. I know you're probably upset, but tomorrow night— No, not tomorrow night, I've got a—a business meeting. Friday night? Will that suit you? I'll pick you up, and we can grill a couple of steaks and enjoy a nice, quiet musical evening at home, just the two of us, getting to know each other."

Jay was no longer sure she wanted to get to know him, but she didn't want to just blurt that out. It wasn't entirely his fault the evening had ended so disastrously. These things happened. She told him not to feel guilty.

"Guilty! Look, just forget it, okay? We'll both just forget it."

He might. She thought it would be a long time before she could forget that ugly, forlorn old mutt.

"Friday night at seven, then," he said.

"Mike, I don't know... I've got this exhibit thing at school—why don't we just let it ride for now?"

She'd give her two-inch sable brush and a ream of three-hundred-pound d'Arches to be back in her studio, with Thad and his baggy old khakis and his scratched glasses talking about Bronze Age burial mounds at Borum Esno, and female fertility figurines from somewhere in France.

Mike got out to see her to the door, and reluctantly she let him walk with her, his arm around her waist. "Well. Thanks for everything," she said, but he shook his head.

"Oh, no. We're not leaving it like that. It's my fault things didn't pan out tonight. I figure I owe you something for that, so we'll just put this down on account, shall we? You can collect the balance of what I owe you on Friday night."

So he kissed her. And she let him, because it had been an awful evening, all things considered, yet it really wasn't Mike's fault. Not all of it. And he was handsome, and she was flattered he'd even taken her out once, much less asked her out again, and she couldn't figure out why he bothered and wished he hadn't, which made her feel guilty.

So she let him kiss her, and she kissed him back, and found herself wondering what Thad's kisses would be like.

Which was crazy! They didn't have that sort of relationship. Theirs was strictly business. Landlady and tenant.

Well . . . maybe a little more than that.

"Until Friday, then," Mike murmured next to her ear, and Jay realized that the kiss had ended and she hadn't even noticed.

"Until Friday," she repeated with a sigh and let herself inside.

7

Thad stood at the front window and watched the low headlights swing into the driveway. He hadn't deliberately waited up for her—actually, he'd expected her to be later than this. He just happened to be unusually restless tonight, that was all.

Outside, a car door shut quietly, then another one opened and shut. So he was seeing her to the door.

And coming inside for a nightcap?

For a nightcap and what else?

He heard the sound of the front door, and then he heard Weems's car start up and drive off, leaving an unnecessary amount of rubber on her driveway.

No hanky-panky, then. Maybe a kiss or two, but nothing that would land her in any serious trouble.

He swore silently. What the hell business was it of his who she kissed, or who she slept with, for that matter? Nothing in his lease precluded a few extracurricular activities on his landlady's part.

His, either, for that matter.

All of which, Thad told himself, was a pretty clear indication that too much time spent as a human source collector—the department's term for a spook on the ground as opposed to one in the sky—could lead to some pretty nasty habits.

He had already turned away when he heard the unmistakable sound of a sob. Hanging on to the banister, he raced down the stairs without giving himself time to think that it was purely none of his business— much less that at his age and in his condition, a guy could break something vital by taking the stairs three at a time.

"Jay," he said awkwardly when she turned to see what the ruckus was all about.

She sniffed. Her eyes were streaming. Her nose was red. He found it endearing, which was a pretty good indication that he'd left his brain in drydock. "Yes— I'm sorry, did you need something?"

Yeah, he needed his head examined. "I heard you come in. That is, I was still awake and I thought I heard—hey, are you all right? That clown didn't try anything, did he?"

Wordlessly, she shook her head. Something was wrong—bad wrong. It was none of his business, whatever it was, but hell, he'd never been able to watch a woman cry without feeling as if he'd eaten broken glass.

He moved a step closer. She held her ground, making no effort to cover her distress. "It's—it was only— we hit a dog. In the car, I mean." Her voice wavered over half an octave, and then she visibly stiffened her shoulders. "It was only a stray—there was no collar—and I think he must have died instantly, but—"

But even so, it had ripped her up pretty bad. Tough, independent, invincible Ms. Turner. Thad lifted his arms instinctively, wanting to hold her until she stopped looking so devastated, but something told him it would be a mistake. For both of them.

God, the woman got to him! The crazy thing was, she wasn't even his type. If he even had a type. Which he didn't.

"Where did it happen?" he asked quietly, and she sniffed, fumbled in her bag for a rumpled tissue and blew her elegant pink-tipped nose.

She told him, described the scene and said she'd dragged the poor animal off the street. "I'd better call the animal control people. I d-d-don't even know if they're the proper ones to c-c-call. He looked hungry. I don't think he'd been eating regularly." Her chin wobbled, and it was all Thad could do not to reach out for her. But before he could, she turned away and hurried off in the direction of her bedroom.

It was purely by accident that she saw the neat mound of fresh earth out near the birdbath the next afternoon. She'd been headed out to the potting shed to leave a box of supplies she'd brought from school when she'd spotted the bones. Big ones. Bleached of all color. One at the head of the oval mound, one at the foot.

Dropping her box of supplies, she sat in the doorway of the shed and cried until her throat hurt, for no real reason at all. A stray dog—a thoughtful professor—it was nothing, really nothing—he'd buried the poor dog in her yard, that was all. You'd think he'd offered her a trip to the Sorbonne and all the chocolate ice cream she could eat.

Jay was tied up at school on Friday until nearly dark. Work in the studio went undone, and she called Mike and explained that she was really pushed to the limit at the moment, but perhaps they could get together after the school term ended.

So that was the end of her birthday gift from the girls, she told herself. She couldn't even say it had been nice while it lasted, because in the end, it had been a waste of time. Time that could have been spent in far more productive ways.

When it came to the games between men and women, Jay was a third-string player, at best. The only S/DWM out of the entire batch who'd even been in her league was Sam from the bookstore.

Which was a pretty dismal thought.

On Saturday, after hauling the last load of junk to the dump and bringing back an armload of eucalyptus someone had pruned and left in a battered coffeepot for anyone who wanted it, Jay stopped by the hardware store and bought a gallon of cheap white latex and a new roller. The walls in the shed had never been painted, and even with the windows cleared, the room was too dark.

She arranged the eucalyptus in a majolica pot on the hall table and hurried back out. It was already past noon, and she wanted to get one coat of paint rolled on before it got too late.

Dragging her stepladder in through the door, she half expected Thad to barge in and insist on helping her. Not that she needed any help, but she was getting used to having some if she wanted it.

When he didn't show up, she refused to admit, even to herself, that she was disappointed. She hadn't seen him for almost three days. Three whole days! If it weren't for the daily food deliveries and the occasional sound of running water upstairs, she might even have worried about him.

Not that she needed his constant interference. Goodness, if there was one thing she couldn't stand, it was someone who insisted on poking his nose in her business. She'd lived alone for too long to put up with that aggravation.

The floor of the shed was a mess. She made a mental note to watch the dump for a usable rug. A light-colored straw mat would be perfect, but that was too much to hope for.

Maybe she'd paint the floor white, too…except that it would take enamel, and enamel was expensive, and besides, it probably wouldn't stick to the place that stayed damp over near the corner, anyway.

Jay brought her boom box out for company while she finished up the second coat Sunday afternoon. WUNC was doing a Greig concerto when she dragged the ladder to the far corner and braced the back legs against the wall.

She was more than halfway up, armed with a pan and a dripping roller, when the back legs suddenly broke through the floor, throwing her off balance. Trying desperately to save herself, she grabbed the ledge over the window, but the wood was old. Frantic, she felt her fingers slip just as the ladder struck the window and collapsed.

She fell in a tangle, one leg through the rungs, one outside.

"Oh, damn, damn, damn," she gasped when she could catch her breath. Gingerly, she flexed the leg that was draped over the side of the ladder. Every inch of her body ached, but at least nothing seemed to be broken. What on earth would happen to her if she ever broke anything? She wouldn't even be able to drive to school!

But things were bad enough even without broken bones. The floor was going to have to be patched before she could move in, and Jay's carpentry skills, while adequate for most things, weren't up to structural repairs. Which meant she would have to hire it done, which would cost a fortune. And thanks to hurricanes and spotted owls, lumber cost a fortune these days, too. "Oh, damn, damn, *damn!*"

She could have wept when she saw what was left of the paint spilling out across the floor. She could have wept anyway, as various scrapes and bruises began to make themselves felt.

Just when she'd hoped to finish up and move in so that she could start painting again. Oh, God, she'd never been so mad in her life!

From across the yard, she heard the front door open and close. A moment later, Thad's voice called her name. "Jay—phone call!"

She closed her eyes and fought against the hysterical urge to laugh. So much for her fancy answering machine. "Let the machine take it!" she called back.

Was that her voice? She sounded as if she'd landed on her vocal cords.

Just then, the ladder, which had been leaning at a grotesque angle against the wall, collapsed in a noisy heap. Several large shards of glass fell to the floor and shattered.

"Sorry, but I was about to make a call when it rang and I picked it up without think— What the bloody hell is going on?"

"I call it Painted Lady with Broken Ladder." She glared at him, fighting tears. "What the devil do you think is going on."

Kneeling beside her, Thad checked out the major bones for breakage. She had a cut on one leg, but other than that, she seemed to be intact. She was hurting like hell and too stubborn to admit it.

"Ouch! I told you there's nothing wrong with me!"

"Be still or I'll tell you what's wrong with you," he growled. "Trust me. You don't want to hear it."

By the time he got her to the house, she was swearing brokenly and obviously wishing him to the ends of the earth.

"I can take care of it myself," she snapped when he eased her ruined sneaker off and examined her foot. Tarsals were pretty delicate, hers more than most.

"Does this hurt? No? Good. I'll go back out and board up your broken window once I get you settled, in case it rains again before you can get it reglazed."

"The window..."

"Ladder caught it on the way down." He was sorry he'd mentioned it. He couldn't remember seeing a more defeated look on a woman's face, not in a long time.

"Maybe we'd better have a medic check you out," he said. Once inside, under a decent light, it was pretty obvious that she wasn't in as good shape as she claimed to be. Her skin was the color of skimmed milk, making her handful of freckles stand out like flecks of rust.

"No."

"Jay, be reasonable. I can have you at the emergency room in—"

"No."

"Okay, but there's no way you're going to be able to clean the paint out of your hair and get out of those ruined clothes without help. You'll have to settle for me, and I'm no great shakes as a lady's maid." The truth was, he wasn't sure he could maintain his objectivity. He was beginning to think he was more shaken that she was. First the thing with the bees, now this.

"I don't need your help, but thanks for offering. If you'll dial 555-7174 and ask for Sue, I'd appreciate it very m-m-much."

He left her fighting tears and trying hard not to show it. He felt like holding her until she'd cried out all her hurt, holding her until every bruise and cut had healed, and then he felt like—

God, there was no fool like an old fool.

Leaving her perched on the kitchen stool, with paint drying on her hair, her face—on almost every visible portion of her body, Thad went to make the call. She'd be safer with another person in the house.

And so would he.

Before she could compose herself, he was back. "No answer. I left a message asking her to call."

Jay considered trying to reach Sara or C.A., but it was Sunday afternoon. C.A. would be doing something with her husband. Sara would be out with her long-term lover. She'd thought maybe Sue and her Gus might be home playing chess, but evidently they'd gone out, too.

Everyone had someone. Everyone but her. Dammit, pain always did this to her—turned her into a whining, sniveling, self-pitying wimp! No wonder she didn't have anyone!

Thad insisted on running her a warm bath and helping ease her out of her clothes, and she accepted because she was such a painty mess, and because she was beginning to ache dreadfully.

He took off his glasses. She didn't know if that was a good sign or a bad sign. At that point, she was past caring.

But he'd definitely been right about one thing. Lifting her arms to wash her hair hurt like the very devil. Evidently, she'd landed on her hip and her elbow and wrenched every muscle in her body on the way down.

There'd been a time in her life when she could fall from the tallest tree on the farm and walk away without a whimper. Len had taught her how to relax and roll with the fall the first time he'd caught her up on the roof, getting ready to fly.

The trouble was, this time she hadn't had time to relax on the way down. She'd have to see about getting a taller ladder.

Thad was waiting when she emerged. Jay didn't want to think about how disappointed she would have been if he'd been gone. That shook her even more than the fall.

"You didn't have to wait, I'm fine. The scratch on my leg was nothing—three Band-Aids covered it just fine. Other than that, there are only a few bumps and bruises, but nothing that won't heal in a day or so."

His gaze moved over her body as if to check out the damage himself, and she watched in amazement as a ruddy color stained his rugged features. "I sent out for

Mexican," he said gruffly. "I didn't think to ask if you liked it, but if you'd rather have something else—"

"Mexican's fine." Anything was fine. She didn't think she could eat a bite, but he was being so decent, not yelling at her for being stupid the way Ronnie would have done. He hadn't even leered at the sight of her lacy underwear when he'd helped ease off her painty clothes.

So she happened to have a weakness for feminine underwear. It was nothing to be ashamed of. Just because she usually wore grungy, paint-stained clothes on the outside didn't mean she was a total slob. It only meant she was practical. Sooner or later, everything she wore that showed—and some that didn't—ended up being dragged across her palette.

Now, dressed in her favorite caftan, she resisted touching the bruise that was beginning to form on her left cheek. Briefly, she'd considered powdering it and had given up the idea as sheer vanity.

If she'd worn makeup, Thad would know she'd done it for his benefit. She had more pride than that.

"Sore?" he asked in that tough-tender tone of voice that made her want to lay all her worries on his shoulders and throw herself into his arms.

"Not really." Actually, the only part of her body that didn't hurt was her hair. She'd gathered it up in a wet bundle and tied it back with a yellow silk scarf, which would probably slither off as soon as it dried. She had that kind of hair. Straight as a stick, slick as boiled okra.

The Mexican dinners were delivered, and Jay thought about getting her purse and paying her share but decided it could wait. He had that bulldog look on his face, and she didn't need the hassle.

Thad placed the two foam containers on the table and got out cutlery and napkins. She would rather have eaten off a plate, but that would mean dish-washing afterward, and she didn't think his solicitude would stretch quite that far.

"I made ice tea," he said as she gingerly shifted to ease her bruised hip. "I'm afraid it's only instant."

Having to drink instant tea was the least of her worries.

Morosely, she stared at his broad shoulders while he took out ice trays and filled two glasses. When he turned around and caught her looking at him, he hesitated. For one long moment, their eyes clung. Jay felt as if some important message passed between them, but when he spoke it was only to ask, "Do you know what the oldest folk cure in the world is?"

Shaking free of his mesmerizing spell, she took a wild guess. "Moldy bread?"

"Kissing. Didn't your mother ever teach you that kissing makes it better?"

Jay swallowed half a chile relleno and felt the heat rise to her face. "Is that a scientific thing, or just something you picked up from poking around in old boneyards?"

He shrugged. "It sounds like more fun than moldy bread."

With a withering look, she returned her attention to her dinner, hoping he wouldn't guess that for a moment she'd visualized him kissing all the scrapes and bruises hidden under her voluminous caftan. She made a mountain of her refried beans and then flattened it out again. Stealing a glance at Thad, she sensed that he was probably every bit as embarrassed as she was.

Honestly! For two middle-aged adults, they were behaving suspiciously like a pair of adolescents.

At least *she* was.

Jay had never suffered any illusions about her looks. Ronnie had seen to that, before the honeymoon was even over.

God, Jay, do you have to wear that awful rag?

Oh for crying out loud, Jay, put on some lipstick, at least! You look like you just came off a three-week bender.

Why don't you try putting on a few more pounds? A friend of mine had a silicone job done on her breasts, and it turned out great! You can't even see the scars.

She'd wanted to ask how he knew, but hadn't quite dared. He'd told her on various occasions that she was as flat as a pool table, that he'd met better-dressed bag ladies and that her neck was too long.

Now, on top of all that, she had wet hair and a black eye, which probably didn't do a whole lot to enhance her feminine allure.

Evidently, looks weren't everything, though. She had dated three different men lately, all of them perfectly acceptable, and the handsomest of the lot had taken her out twice and asked her out a third time. What more could any woman want?

Don't ask, she warned herself silently.

Over the following week, supper together got to be a habit. If Jay allowed herself to enjoy it a little too much, she never lost sight of the danger. Her head might occasionally get lost in the clouds, but fortunately her feet were planted firmly on the ground.

She knew very well that Thad was only a temporary part of her life. In a few months he'd move on, and she would clean the second floor and advertise for another tenant.

While she was at it, she might even place another ad in the personals column. "Widowed schoolteacher is searching for anthropologist with wicked eyes, gentle hands and a body straight off the cover of a romance novel."

The morning after her fall, Jay had been almost too stiff and sore to move, but of course she'd had no choice. Thad had offered to drive her to school and pick her up afterward, which had done more to galvanize her into action than anything else he could have done. The mere thought of being dependent on another person scared the wits out of her. She'd worked too hard for too long to prove to herself that she didn't need anyone else—that she could make it on her own.

But the occasional supper together—that was different. There was no real reason why she should eat alone downstairs while Thad ate alone upstairs. It wasn't a matter of dependence. She could have picked up the phone and ordered in as easily as he could, and anyway, she always insisted on paying her share.

Thad found dozens of ways to help her out. He was there when she got home from school each day, to carry in anything she'd brought home with her. He'd called in a glazier and had the window repaired, which had irritated her because she'd planned to save money by doing it herself.

But when he explained that he'd wanted to do it himself, but that home repairs had never been his long suit, he had cut the wind right out of her sails. For a moment there, he'd sounded almost vulnerable.

He answered the telephone to keep her from having to dash up eight steps, and offered to have new lines installed, with a jack for the kitchen, the bathroom, her bedroom and his study.

"If you're dissatisfied with the accommodations, just say so."

"Did I say I was dissatisfied? Jay, even you have to admit that this place of yours is pretty archaic." He'd found her sprawled on the sofa bed, which was old and soft and easy on bruised bodies.

"I thought you liked old ruins," she shot back. It hurt her when he criticized her house. No it didn't, either. It made her mad as a hornet! "And what do you mean, *even* I?"

"It was merely a figure of speech. Look, I've got nothing against Victorian houses, but this one needs some attention to bring it into the twentieth century if you're going to go on—"

"My house is not Victorian, it happens to be Queen Anne!" At least according to C.A. it was. Jay didn't know the difference, and was pretty sure Thad didn't, either.

"As I was saying, it could stand some modernizing. Nobody has just one phone these days. Especially not when they're renting out space."

"There, I knew you were complaining!"

"Dammit, I'm not complaining. But if you go jumping up every time the damned phone rings, one of these days you're going to break something vital, and I might not be here to pick up the pieces."

"Fine!" she yelled. "That's just fine with me! Your lease will be up on June fifteenth, so maybe you'd better start looking around for someplace with lots of telephones with crazy gadgets hooked up to them, like modems and microwaves and—fax machines!"

Which was so patently ridiculous that she burst into tears.

"Ahhh, Jay... Don't cry, honey. I didn't mean anything by what I said. Personally, I don't even like telephones. But you do need to take better care of yourself. I might not be around next time you take a tumble."

Lifting her face from her arms, she glared at him through a tangle of long wet lashes. "I take excellent care of myself. I've taken excellent care of myself for ten years, thank you. For longer than that.''

"I know you have. You're a warrior of a woman. You're the Statue of Liberty. You're Yakshim, the free spirit." He sat down and drew her into his arms, and like a pot plant needing water, she wilted all over him.

"What I am is silly," she said, sniffing, smearing her tears on his rumpled collar.

"I wouldn't have put it quite like that."

She offered him a watery smile. "I know you wouldn't. You're much too kind. Thad, I'm grateful, I really am, only it means a lot to me—knowing I can take care of myself."

He eased to a more comfortable position until she was leaning back against his chest. The sofa was a king-size sleeper, too old to be fashionable, but too comfortable to be thrown out. "I know how much your independence means to you, Jay. But while I'm here, let me shoulder some of the burden." He laughed, but there was a hollow ring to the sound. "At least I'd like to try. I've never been good at sharing myself—never had much of a chance to learn how. I'd like to think I'm not totally selfish."

If there was one thing she did know about him, it was that he wasn't good at sharing himself—and that the last thing he was, was selfish. Which was two things, but who was counting?

Twisting in his arms, Jay stared up at the deep lines that bracketed his mouth, at the crow's-feet caused by too many years of squinting at foreign suns. There was a small scar just below his angular cheekbone on the left side, and she wondered how he'd got it, and if anyone had offered to kiss it better for him.

"You're a lot of things," she told him, her gaze lingering on his thick, shower-damp hair. A color somewhere between gray and gold and brown, it grew in cowlicks so that it never looked quite groomed. "But I'd never call you selfish."

He took off his glasses and slung them across the coffee table. Without them, his eyes looked almost black. "Then you can't know what I'm thinking right this minute," he said, his quiet voice raising goose-flesh along her flank.

She only hoped it wasn't the same thing she was thinking, because if it was, they were both in trouble.

It was. His hands moved up to cover her breasts and he buried his face in her hair. Jay closed her eyes, knowing that what he wanted was precisely what she wanted, if the feel of his aroused body pressing intimately against her backside was anything to judge by.

She wondered why she wasn't wasn't more surprised. Possibly because it had been in the air, a silent presence between them, ever since she'd fallen off the ladder. Even before that.

She couldn't remember just when it had started—or why—but she had a very good idea where it was going to end.

It was but a few steps to her bedroom. Seeing him against her flowered wallpaper and homemade curtains was a mistake. From this moment on, no matter how many continents separated them, Jay knew he'd be haunting her bedroom. Haunting her heart.

"Are you sure, Jay? I don't want you regretting this tomorrow." He was unbuttoning his shirt, his square-tipped fingers as deft as any surgeon's as they made short work of the task.

"I'm thirty-seven years old, Thad. It's been ten years for me. This is not something I'd ever do without a lot of thought."

Was it her imagination, or did his fingers hesitate then? "Jay, I can't offer you anything more than this. You understand that, don't you?"

"I didn't ask for anything more. You'll leave in a few weeks and I'll still be here. Nothing will have changed—for either of us."

They came together in the middle of the large room—a room that spoke of permanence and commitment and old-fashioned ideals that were as obsolete as the horse and buggy. Holding her away from him, Thad studied her openly. She was tall for a woman, slender to the point of thinness. And touchingly awkward with her own nakedness.

"If you were expecting voluptuousness, I'm afraid you're in for a disappointment." Her smile was tremulous, vulnerable.

"I wasn't expecting anything, Jay. I don't have the right. But you must know how beautiful you are."

Jay felt her smile grow wider, more sure. She wasn't about to argue with him. Whether it was diplomacy or poor eyesight, she'd just as soon he kept his illusions.

"I like the way you look, too," she told him shyly. "That scar on your thigh—it looks new."

"An accident. I've been told it will fade in time."

She touched it and then drew back her hand, watching him uncertainly. It looked suspiciously like a bullet wound. She couldn't conceive of his being shot. Anthropology wasn't a hazardous occupation... was it?

Thad took her hand, opened her fingers and kissed them, one by one, and then he drew her to him and groaned. "I've lain awake nights fantasizing about this—and forgot about the necessity of fumbling around in my wallet for something that might or might not still be there."

Laughing, Jay leaned against him, her arms sliding around his neck. "Me, too. It's been so long for me—"

Between them they managed. They managed beautifully. Thad was a man of infinite patience. He had learned the art of love at an early age and studied extensively in his younger years. Jay brought out every vestige of tenderness he possessed. There was an innocent quality about her that defied logic, considering the fact that she had been married for seven years and widowed for ten.

He knew only that pleasuring her was the most important thing in his life at this moment. If he could bring her joy, even briefly, he would put off his own satisfaction forever.

Patience. It was a quality much to be desired in a lover. Thad was patient by nature and patient by training. Now he used every bit of that patience to make love to her body until she was glowing all over, moaning with pleasure. And he found to his own surprise that his own pleasure was multiplied a hundredfold.

Impulsiveness. It was a quality he had noticed about her before, even though she did her best to suppress it. She was a generous, impulsive lover, and it nearly did him in more than once. When she touched him just so—kissed him just there—something he suspected she had never done before with any man, he nearly lost it.

"Jay, Jay—ah, sweetheart, give me a minute, will you? I want this to be good for you—"

"I'm sorry."

"No, don't apologize! Gad, lady, you set me on fire!" She was lying in his arms, half beside him, half on top of him. Thad figured her husband had been either a eunuch or a fool. "Don't ever apologize to any man. It's just that you're so perfect—so damned sweet—so wonderful—and it's been so long for me."

The inevitable could be postponed no longer. Thad entered her slowly, amazed, even though he had tested her readiness before, at how very tight she was. What a waste, he thought as he sank into her welcoming warmth.

He was trembling, trying not to bear his full weight on her, afraid he would lose control before she was ready, when he felt her begin to convulse around him.

There was no holding back. He drove deep, withdrew slowly, and plunged again, every tendon in his body taut. Then he went wild. With her soft, sweet cries cascading over him, he exploded inside her and collapsed.

Later, he would remember thinking, just before he slept, that this had been the mistake of a lifetime. He wasn't sure why. He only knew that if he had it all to do over again, he wouldn't.

Right. And the sun wouldn't rise in the east again, either.

Jay woke up first. She was smiling. Propping herself up on her elbow, she gazed down at the sleeping man beside her and looked her fill at his face, his tanned throat, the shaggy hair that invited her touch.

She hadn't realized how long and dense his lashes were. For some reason, it made him seem vulnerable, which made her feel like crying.

Her hand was resting on his flat abdomen. Feeling the heat of him, her hand crept lower and then stopped, fingers curling against temptation. If she was smart, she would leave before he woke up. She could be showered and dressed and out in the studio so that he could have some time to himself—time to pull his thoughts together.

If he was as scattered as she was right now, he would appreciate it, Jay told herself. Now that it was already too late.

"I didn't mean to wake you," she whispered.

"You didn't. I was lying here wondering what you were going to do with that hand."

Face flaming, she jerked her hand out from under the sheet and mumbled some excuse about just waking up and not realizing where her hand was.

"Balderdash."

"What?" A gasp of laughter escaped her, and he grinned lazily and reached for his glasses, but they were in the other room on the coffee table.

"It's a three-syllable word that means, if you think I believe that, you've got termites in your brain."

She already knew she had termites in her brain. Making love with Thaddeus Blanchard figured right up there with marrying Ronnie Turner among the major mistakes in her life. Yet she was glad she'd done it, which was how she knew about the termites. No sane woman, knowing she was dangerously attracted to a man who was no more permanent than the morning dew, would have dared do anything so reckless. A week ago they had begun by sharing meals, and then he'd started having a pot of fresh coffee waiting for her when she got home, and bringing in her groceries and her year-end accumulation of junk from school. They had listened to the BBC on his short wave radio, and to her favorite arias from *Lucia* and *Pearlfishers* and *La Bohème*.

Now, as if all that weren't dangerous enough, she'd had to go and share her body with him. To make love with him. And that's what it was. On her part, at least. Making love. Not having sex.

"Who's going to shower first?" she asked brightly, easing her arm from under his.

"There's plenty of time. Jay, tell me about your marriage," he said now in that quiet, compelling voice that melted her bones like candle wax. He began stroking her wrist with his thumb, tracing an area where one of her many bruises had faded to a nasty shade of yellow. Watching, as if the small movement of flesh on flesh was the most fascinating thing in the world, she laughed self-consciously.

"I think there's sort of a trade imbalance going on here, don't you?"

"Meaning?"

"Meaning you know practically everything there is to know about me and all I know about you is that you're an anthropologist who likes pizza with anchovies and—"

"And beautiful ladies who purr when they sleep and get their back up when they think their independence is being threatened."

She started to argue, but he cut her off in the most effective way. This time, Jay thought dazedly, it was almost as if he cared—almost as if he were trying to tell her something. His mouth came down on hers so tenderly, so gently, it was as if their explosive coming together last night had never happened.

Yet the latent power was still there. Was he going to make love to her again? Did she dare risk it?

But this time his kiss was slow and sweet and not at all aggressive. It was almost as if he were telling her he loved her.

Or telling her goodbye.

His lips trailed over her cheek and nuzzled her temple. She thought he sighed. Was he already regretting it?

Oh, she hoped not! Whatever happened in the future—and nothing could. He'd made certain she knew that. But whatever happened, Jay knew she would never regret making love with Thad. All her life she had wondered if there was something wrong with her, some vital part of her that was missing.

Sex had simply never quite lived up to its billing, not even when it had been new and exciting and Ronnie had been on his best behavior.

Until last night. Whatever happened in the future, she could never regret a single moment of what had happened last night.

"Thad, I have to get up," she said drowsily. "I've got a million things to do."

"Tell me you're not sorry?"

She shook her head. "Never. Are you?"

He laughed, and once more she sensed a hollowness in the sound that struck her suddenly as lonely. "Yeah—in a way, I think maybe I am." He kissed the small pucker that appeared between her brows. "I don't want to hurt you. I'd never want to do that," he said, and she was afraid he meant more than a few bruises. Afraid he was referring to the kind of hurt that cut a lot deeper and lasted a lot longer than any minor injuries she might have sustained falling off a ladder.

"Don't worry. You didn't," she said, praying she spoke the truth.

She started to disengage herself from his arms, but before she could do more than slide one foot out from under the covers, the phone rang. The transom over the door was open, and the sound carried quite clearly. After the fourth ring, the message machine took over.

"Jay, it's me, Mike Weems. I just got my car out of the shop, and it's good as new. Hey, since you never returned my call from last Saturday, I figure you might still be upset about what happened. What I'm calling about is, I'd really like a chance to make it up to you. So what about my place? We can toss a couple of steaks on the grill and listen to that music we bought— what do you say?"

8

—◆—

Thad leaned against his car outside the library, watching an impromptu football game played by a dozen or so laughing young men and women. The game had little to do with the pigskin—more to do with scoring.

Did they still call it that?

God, he felt old! A few nights ago, holding Jay in his arms, trying to figure out how to get into her bloomers and whether or not he still had a condom in his wallet, and whether the thing was any good, he'd felt no older than the gangly kid over there in the size-fifteen unlaced hightops, who was doing his damnedest to attract the attention of a shapely young coed in a skirt that barely covered her derriere.

And then one thing had led to another, and he'd wound up in her bed, and now he couldn't seem to get his life back on track. He'd been going under for the third time when Weems had left that latest message and he'd jumped on it the way a drowning man jumps on anything that floats.

Weems. He was young, he was good-looking—he had a lot more potential than a middle-aged anthropologist who occasionally doubled as a spook. But more important, long after Thad had moved on, Weems would still be here.

Jay deserved someone young, someone personable—a guy who stood a chance of putting down roots and making them grow. Because Jay was a roots woman. She could never be satisfied living the nomadic kind of existence he'd led all his life.

With a fleeting sense of regret, Thad told himself that Weems just might fill the bill. Evidently she thought so, too. She'd gone out with him more than once.

Of course, Thad had conveniently forgotten to tell her about one of his calls from last week, but if the guy couldn't take a little discouragement, he didn't deserve a woman like Jay Turner. Above all, she needed a man who would appreciate her.

Sliding into his car, Thad started up the engine and pulled out of the parking lot, trying to ignore the mating games being played on the nearby lawn. All his instincts were telling him it was time to bug out. Time to regroup and rethink before he got in any deeper.

The fact that he didn't *want* to bug out—that he didn't want to think—that all he wanted to do was race back to that decaying pile of cupolas and gingerbread, take his landlady back to bed and keep her there until neither one of them had the strength to move again, was proof enough that he was on a steep, slippery slope.

Thad told himself that the occasional case of horniness was only to be expected in a healthy male who'd been celibate too long. He was only forty-one years old, for crying out loud. Forty-one wasn't exactly over the hill.

Ignoring the remarks about her fading shiner—she had told her classes exactly how it had happened to stop the rumors before they could get started—Jay concentrated on winding up the school year. And then she concentrated on not spending more than thirty minutes out of any one hour thinking about Thad. May as well get into training for when he left. Because sooner or later he would. That had been understood from the very first.

Maybe she would return Mike's call after all. Maybe a night on the town with the delectable would-be dentist was exactly what she needed.

She still hadn't figured out just why *he* seemed to need *her*. Both times she'd gone out with him they'd run into women who knew him and who, judging from the way they'd looked at him, wouldn't mind knowing him even better. They were all older women, too—anywhere from late thirties to mid-forties, at a guess, and all attractive and assured in a way she had never been.

"Mike, what is it with all these women?" she'd asked him the night of the concert.

"Women? What women? I don't see any women."

"How about the redhead in khaki and black silk sitting on the aisle. I thought she was going to lasso you with her purse strap when we passed by." Jay had been teasing, but she'd been curious, too. She was pretty sure he was at least a decade younger than most of the women who ogled him. The more she saw of him, the more she was certain he'd lied about his age as well as a few other matters.

"Oh, her. Just someone I know casually. We, uh—live in the same apartment complex."

So Jay returned his call, telling herself that the flattering attentions of a handsome, charming if somewhat insensitive young man were better than any geriatric multivitamin when it came to maintaining a healthy ego. It had nothing to do with the fact that she was more than half in love with a man who was going to walk away without a backward glance.

She got his machine and left a message to say she was returning his call. Before she even reached the bottom of the stairs, her phone rang, and she raced back up.

"Jay? It's Mike." He sounded breathless. The music in the background sounded like Ravel. "Does it strike you that our phone calls are beginning to resemble a tennis match?"

"Well, now that you mention it..."

"My serve, I believe," he teased.

He really was charming, she told herself, in spite of the flash of temper he'd revealed the night he'd run into that poor dog. Not to mention a few other minor flaws—but then, who was she to demand perfection?

She dismissed as sheer heresy the fleeting thought that she'd be far more comfortable sharing take-out food with a shaggy old lecturer who hid a wicked grin behind a pair of scratchy glasses and a perfectly splendid body under baggy old clothes.

The next evening Mike picked her up in his flashy red sports car, looking like a male model fresh off a beach assignment.

Or fresh from a tanning salon.

"Hey, lady, you look like a breath of spring tonight," he told her, which, while not particularly original, was nice to hear. "I left the wine breathing and the steaks out on the counter, ready to grill."

"That sounds lovely." It occurred to her that much more of this kind of treatment and she'd forget how to cook. And while cooking for one was not much fun, it was a part of the discipline she'd imposed on herself after Ronnie had died. Her mother called it keeping up appearances. Jay called it maintaining standards, because appearances had never been all that important to her.

But standards *were* important, and she knew that once she started letting things slide, it would be all too easy to slip into bad habits. So up until a week ago, she had cooked at least five nights a week and served herself on the cloth-covered table, using her blue willowware and Great-Aunt Ruth's old-fashioned silver instead of merely slapping a paper plate and a handful of stainless-steel cutlery onto the vinyl-topped service bar.

Somehow, she didn't think Mike Weems, with his yellow sharkskin slacks and his sexy black shirt open to reveal the heavy gold pendant on a leather thong, would appreciate her turnip greens, sweet potato biscuits and boiled shoulder, no matter how she served it.

As Mike consistently drove well over the speed limit, the drive didn't take long. He pulled into the apartment parking lot with a flourish, favored her with another smoldering look and leaned over to open her door, pressing his arm against her breasts in the process.

Jay hoped it was an accident, but suspected it wasn't. She began to wonder if she was sending the wrong signals by agreeing to dinner for two in a man's apartment.

As for the apartment itself, it had all the personality of a department store furniture display. Somehow, that didn't come as any great surprise—although to be perfectly fair, Mike was only subleasing. Just because she happened to prefer something more traditional . . .

And he really was remarkably handsome. And charming. Except for his driving. But then, everyone drove over the speed limit these days. Most people. At least some people.

"What d'you think? Pretty cool, huh?"

She assured him that it was pretty cool, dusted her fingerprint off a black lacquered table, then surreptitiously used her skirt to wipe off the smear she'd made. The room resembled a movie set, with Mike as the male lead. Which made her...what? The comic relief?

Mike poured two glasses of wine, which was a red. Jay wasn't partial to reds, but even she knew better than to expect a sophisticate like Mike Weems to serve white wine with steaks.

Actually, she would have preferred sweetened ice tea, but she wasn't gauche enough to say so. Anyway, red was supposed to be good for the heart or the arteries or something. What was that old saying about a million Frenchmen couldn't be wrong?

Or was that about snails?

Sipping the tart wine, she turned away to hide her grimace, pretending to study the wall art. It reminded her of the wiring schematic on the back of her washing machine.

"Nice, hmm? I especially like the one over the sofa."

It was another schematic, possibly of a giant toaster complete with heating coils. She allowed herself to be led across the room for a closer look.

"You know, the interesting thing about this one is that it looks entirely different depending on your viewing angle. Now if you were to lie down on the sofa—"

"Oh, there's another one," she exclaimed. Moving away, she pretended an interest in a horizontal version of the same schematic over the fake fireplace. Evidently they came as a set. Amused at his transparent ploy, she wondered if there was a fourth one in the bedroom. A ceiling painting, perhaps?

Surely he didn't think she was that naive. Probably his idea of a joke, she thought as he turned away to fiddle with the controls on a stack of black-on-black boxes that looked as if they belonged in a laboratory.

A moment later the room filled with the strains of some subtly insistent refrain. Jay tried to place it and gave up. It didn't sound like the *Bolero*. And it certainly didn't sound Irish!

Mike stepped out of his loafers and invited Jay to step out of hers, and in deference to the white rugs, she did. And then wished she hadn't. Which was strange, because she usually stepped out of her shoes the minute she got home.

"Are we going to eat soon?" she asked in an effort to break the strange tension that seemed to be building as a direct result of the music. "Is there something I can do to help?"

"The steaks need to reach room temp before I toss 'em on the grill. We could always pass the time by dancing," he murmured, sliding both arms around her waist and leaning his forehead against hers. The music was sensuous and insistent. A slow drumbeat and an alto sax. Saxophones, for reasons Jay had never fully understood, always seemed to affect her internal organs. This one was lethal.

"That's not one of the records we bought, is it?" she asked.

"This one's from my personal collection."

"Oh. Um—what is it?" she asked after a few more minutes of dancing in slow, slow motion.

"Would you believe Sousa?"

Which made her laugh, which momentarily eased the wariness that had begun stealing over her the moment she'd stepped into his parlor.

But not for long. By the time they got around to grilling steaks and tossing a salad, Jay was wondering what had happened to her sense of survival. Sure, a healthy ego was important, but not as important as common sense. Whatever small store of common sense she had once possessed seemed to have evaporated over the past few days.

The salad was good. She'd tossed it herself. But the steak was rare, in spite of the fact that she had told Mike distinctly that she liked hers well-done. It didn't help matters when he insisted on feeding her, cutting off forksful of shiny red meat, holding cherry tomatoes in his fingers for her to bite in half and then finishing them himself, all the while smiling at her in a heavy-lidded way that made her wonder if he was troubled by allergies.

"Do you have any idea what you do to me?" he asked, his voice the consistency of chocolate syrup.

"Goodness, would you look at the time!" she said brightly. Crumpling her napkin beside her plate, she tried to rise, but Mike was too fast for her. He moved behind her chair, leaned over to nuzzle her ear and whispered something she wanted to believe she had misunderstood.

"I beg your pardon?"

His laughter was low and throbbing, as if he were trying to imitate the pulsating beat of the music. The same piece had been playing over and over while they'd been eating. By no stretch of the imagination would Jay have described it as dinner music.

"I've got an idea—why don't we explore the rest of the apartment and see if we can't find somewhere more comfortable to relax?"

"I've got an even better idea. Why don't we listen to the album I picked out the other night? I think you'd really like it if you gave it a chance."

"Album. That's quaint. You know, Jay, you're really sweet."

"CD, then. You know what I mean." She leaned away from him, but he was too quick and too agile. Lowering his face, he nibbled the place on her neck that was most sensitive, and she shoved his head away. "Mike, is that what this is all about? Is that why you brought me here?"

He managed to look hurt, but it was such a patently false effort that she suspected he practiced before a mirror. The thought amused her enough that in spite of her irritation she had to smile.

"How much do I owe you for dinner? The salad was wonderful, but I wish now I'd turned the steak back out onto the range. It might even have survived."

He sat up and smoothed back his hair. "What the hell are you bitching about?"

"I think we both know what's going on here. I'm perfectly willing to pay for my supper, Mike, but I don't play the kind of games you're obviously interested in."

"Jay, Jay. Look, you've got me all wrong, baby."

"No, I think I've got you all right. Finally. Sorry I'm such a slow learner. I'm also sorry you wasted so much time on me."

Suddenly she was reminded of her youngest sister, who always used to poke out her lower lip when she didn't get her way. Len always told her she was going to trip over it if she didn't haul it back in, which only made matters worse.

Gently, Jay said, "Look, Mike, if I'd known you expected—"

"Why did you place that ad if you didn't mean it?"

"What do you mean, if I didn't mean it? All it said was that I liked art and gardening and—"

"You know what I mean!"

"No, actually, I don't." She could have told him she hadn't placed the ad, but that was irrelevant. She had used it. She'd accepted dates with three of the respondents.

"Look, sweetheart, for your information, if all I'd wanted was companionship, I'd have joined a damn club. We both know what those ads are all about."

"Judging from the ones I've read, different people want different things. Friendship. Companionship. Shared interests. A few even hinted at a serious relationship."

"So? Isn't that what I'm talking about?"

Her smile was the same one she used on her older kids who thought they could get around her with some fantastic tale about why their term project wasn't finished—or even begun. "I don't think so, Mike. I don't even think you'd understand my idea of a serious relationship."

"What's to understand? I took you to a movie, we went out to dinner, I took you to a concert and an art exhibit. Does that look like a guy who's only interested in jumping into the sack?"

"You were married once. What did you have in mind when you asked your wife to marry you?"

"Are you crazy? You thought I wanted to *marry* you?"

As depressing as the situation was, Jay had to laugh. No wonder this male child never graduated from dental college. She had sixteen-year-olds who were more mature.

"May I use your phone to call a cab?"

"I'll take you home," he muttered sullenly, but Jay only smiled and shook her head. His driving was hazardous enough when he was in a good mood. Testosterone and temper tantrums were a dangerous combination.

But before she could call for a ride, the phone rang. Mike flung himself off the sofa, grumbling something about ungrateful women.

Although just what she was supposed to be grateful for, Jay wasn't sure. She didn't care for rare steak or red wine, and she hadn't even got to hear the CD she'd picked out.

She was looking for a phone book to get the number of the cab company when Mike muttered something about seeing someone later and hung up the phone. "May I?" she asked politely.

"Be my guest," he snarled.

Which was precisely what she didn't want to be.

Five minutes later she was standing outside the front of the complex, under the bright pink sodium vapor light, waiting for a cab when someone called her name. Startled, she spun around. "Sue? What on earth are you doing here?"

"Visiting. More to the point, what are you doing here? Didn't you get my message?"

"What message?"

"I told you I've got this friend who lives here in Mike's apartment complex. Well, she happened to pick up a newspaper he left out by the pool the other day, and the personal section was full of checks and X marks, all for S/DWFs in the thirty-to-forty-something range. The word is, he's got this thing about older women being better lovers because they're grateful for the attention or some weird thing, and if his checks and X marks mean anything, he's already gone through half the women in Orange County."

A taxi pulled up to the curb. Sue took a couple of bills from her purse and sent him on his way. "Come on, hon, I'll take you home. You're gonna get a good eyeball-to-eyeball lecture, because you obviously don't listen to your phone messages."

Jay folded herself into Sue's red compact, and her friend wheeled out onto Jones Ferry Road as if it were an extension of the Wilkesboro Speedway. "Sue! I'm not wearing a helmet!"

"Sorry. We ate Mexican tonight. It always revs me up. Hey, Jay—I'm sorry about the ad, too. I reckon the whole thing was a fiasco, but it seemed like a good idea at the time. Number two wasn't so bad, was he?"

"Neither was Sam. But don't do me any more favors, will you?" In retrospect, the whole thing was more comical than tragic, but even so, it was hardly flattering. "I hope that's the end of the lecture. I don't think my ego can stand much more."

"Not quite. It seems the jerk's got this 'three strikes and you're out' system. He'll give a woman three chances, and if she doesn't put out for him—"

"Sue, that's so crude!"

"'Scuse me. If she doesn't surrender her virtue to him, he dumps her—is that better?"

"Three chances, you say? Thank God I struck out before that little wretch warmed up his best pitches." Jay closed her eyes and leaned her head back against the headrest. "Sue, d'you think thirty-seven is too young for menopause?"

"Mood swings? Hot flushes?"

"No—well, maybe mood swings. What I'm wondering is where's all that famous wisdom that's supposed to come with age? The only thing I've gotten good at is making a fool of myself. Over and over and over." And the most humiliating part of all was that Thad had been right there to witness, if not actually participate in, every pathetic episode.

Sue pulled into the driveway. Leaving the motor running, she turned to Jay and said, "Hey, don't take it to heart, doll—life's a messy business. Take my advice—dig in and enjoy."

It was too much to hope that Thad wouldn't be waiting up. Honestly, he was getting to be worse than her own conscience.

"You're early," he said.

She shrugged. "Headache," she said, and realized it wasn't merely a convenient excuse. Not that she owed him an explanation.

"You had a call earlier. Someone named Sue. She left a message."

Jay prayed for a convenient trapdoor to open up under her feet. Unfortunately, the only trapdoor in the house was on the ceiling of the second floor, leading to the third-floor attic.

"Yes, well—I'm sorry if you were disturbed."

Something in the way he was looking at her led her to believe that he was more than disturbed—he was embarrassed. For her, probably. Which made two of them.

"Are you all right?" he asked softly.

Instantly, Jay's backbone stiffened. "I'm perfectly all right, and now, if you'll excuse me—"

"Actually, something's come up. I'm afraid I'm going to have to ask a favor of you."

They were still standing in the foyer. Her feet were fused to the worn Bokhara rug, or else she would have long since fled the scene. He wanted out of his lease, she thought, wondering if hearts actually fractured.

Lifting her chin, she managed to smile. "So go ahead—ask. I certainly owe you one." In the glow of the small table lamp, she could see the shadows and planes of his angular features. He had a strong nose. Funny, she'd never before realized what an asset a strong nose on a man could be. Ronnie's nose had been even smaller than her own. Mike's was small, too, and a little too perfect. Everything about him was a little too perfect. Except for his character.

"Well?" she asked just before his gaze captured hers and made a mockery of her act of disinterest.

Moving closer, he suddenly reached out and tucked a length of escaped hair behind her ear, his hand lingering on her cheek. "Velvet," he murmured. "It has something to do with freckles."

She was hallucinating again. He'd been about to ask a favor, but it didn't seem to matter, because his eyes were saying something altogether different, anyway.

Something that made her hopes rise against all reason, against all common sense.

When he took another step closer, she stood her ground, wanting him more than she had ever wanted anything in her life—needing him even more than that.

The kiss started out as a gentle salute, but within seconds it exploded into a white-hot inferno of sexual need that fed on itself, demanding total surrender. Until two nights ago, Jay had never known how devastatingly beautiful sex between two people could be. What was there about this one man in all the world that made her react to him the way she did? He wasn't handsome. He wasn't even particularly young. His sense of style was even worse than her own.

It had nothing to do with his looks, and yet she would rather spend the rest of her life looking at him than spend one hour in heaven.

His tongue explored her mouth and he groaned and dragged her closer, making her vibrantly aware of his arousal. With the whole house at their disposal, they were standing beside the front door like a couple of kids sneaking one last good-night kiss. And instead of trying to hang on to her sanity—to hang on to a single shred of dignity—she was practically climbing all over him.

The only thing that made it even bearable, she thought distractedly when she could think once more, was the fact that he was just as reckless as she was. Gradually, their breathing grew less ragged. Thad leaned his hips against the hall table and drew her against him. "Jay, my sweet Jaybird—do you have any notion how ridiculous a man my age feels trying to make out in the front hall?"

She had somehow come to be wedged between his thighs. It was an incredibly intimate position. She made an effort to disengage herself, but his arms tightened around her. Nor was there any noticeable lessening of interest in other parts of his body. He shifted his weight, which had the effect of bringing her in even more intimate contact, and then he tucked her head under his jaw and wiggled his chin against her scalp.

Having surrendered all control of her body, Jay struggled for control of her mind. Nothing had changed, she thought helplessly. Even knowing he was no more interested in a permanent relationship than Mike had been, she had only to look at him to fall apart.

Gathering her courage, she said calmly, "You said you had a favor to ask?" She could sense his withdrawal, even though his arms still held her. His hand was still on her breast, which meant he could feel her heart pounding like a cage full of wild birds.

"What favor?" She asked when he remained silent. He had to know she would have walked through fire if he'd asked her to. Or was that one of those native rites that anthropologists took for granted?

"The thing is, I seem to have acquired myself a houseguest. I didn't invite her—wasn't expecting her, but she showed up and... Well, to cut to the chase, I told her she could stay for a few days." He peered uneasily at her face, and when she began to withdraw, he let her go.

"So that's why you were waiting for me," she said quietly.

"Not entirely. I was concerned after I heard that messa—"

Jay cut him off. "Invite as many guests as you want. It's nothing to do with me."

"Jay? Are you sure?"

"Of course I'm sure. You didn't even have to ask, but I appreciate your courtesy."

Courtesy be damned. She wanted to hit him! She wanted to kick his shins and bloody that strong nose of his and see how much *he* enjoyed hurting!

"Naturally, I expect to pay extra to cover any additional utilities."

She must have made some suitable comment. Walking away, her back straight, her head high and her fingers tearing the strap of her purse to shreds, Jay's mind was seething.

Her. She. After all that had happened between them, Thad had a woman sharing his apartment!

Belatedly, she tried to steel herself against the pain, but this time the wound cut too deep. This time something far more vital than her poor battered ego was at stake.

9

In her stubborn refusal to climb out of her safe, comfortable rut, Jay had occasionally been accused of having tunnel vision. If having tunnel vision was the same as being goal oriented, she was determined to put it to good use. Deliberately ignoring the existence of Thad and his houseguest, she set herself the task of finishing her studio and moving in. She didn't care if he installed a whole harem on the second floor of her house as long as they kept out of her way.

Oh, yes, she did, too, but that was her problem, not his. If she ignored it long enough, it would eventually go away.

By the time the carpenter she'd hired loaded his tools into his pickup and drove off, one hundred twelve dollars and seventy-three cents richer, Jay was almost too tired to move. While he'd ripped out and replaced the corner flooring where the leaking roof had rotted it out, she had finished hauling the rest of her paraphernalia from her old studio to her new one and putting it away.

With any luck, by this time tomorrow she'd be one canvas closer to her one-woman show.

At the moment, however, she was too tired to gloat. Too tired, too filthy and too hungry. She hadn't stopped to eat lunch, and breakfast was ancient history.

Opening her tiny, half-empty freezer, she took inventory. One TV dinner that had been in there for at least two years. One chicken breast, half a pound of coffee—a loaf of bread and one pork chop. A ham bone she'd been saving for soup and half a dozen packages of blackberries she'd picked in case she ever got around to making another cobbler.

In other words, nothing. She didn't have enough energy to thaw anything, let alone cook it. She wasn't even sure she could drum up the energy to climb the eight steps to order out, but it was either that or settle for cold cereal. Considering the fact that she'd expended roughly a gazillion calories today, she owed herself something more exciting than raisin bran.

She ordered pizza. Loaded. Then she headed to the bathroom to run herself an Olympic-size hot bath, where she intended to soak her poor aching body until her bones melted or her pizza was delivered, whichever came first.

"What happened to all my hot water?" she wailed five minutes later.

Thad's woman.

Fuming, Jay hastily dunked and scrubbed in the lukewarm bath, dried herself quickly and threw on her caftan. Not bothering to glance in the mirror, she marched into her old studio, the room now depressingly empty, and scowled up at the register.

He had covered it with a rug. Great. Why couldn't he have done it before she'd gone to all the trouble and expense of moving out?

"Thad! I need to speak to you!" she yelled up at the painted grill overhead. "Thad?"

Upstairs, someone searched the FM dial at full volume and settled on a top ten station. The sound of a six-car pileup accompanied by the scream of an electric guitar assaulted her ears.

With an ominous gleam in her eye, Jay headed for the back stairs, taking them two at a time. "Thaddeus? I need to talk to you!"

A head full of red hair bristling with jumbo pink rollers poked out the door to her right. "I think he's across the hall working on his old papers. Who are you?"

Jay glared at the redhead who was clutching a mascara wand in one silver-taloned fist. "Dr. Blanchard's landlady. Would you mind telling me what happened to the hot water?" Oh, for heaven's sake, even with all that war paint, the little twit looked barely old enough to vote. What *was* it with men, anyway? Older women, younger women—why couldn't they stick to playing in their own league?

"Gee, I dunno—has something happened to it? There was plenty when I took my bath and washed my hair and rinsed out a few things. Teddy always showers in the morning. Of course, sometimes he showers at night, too, if we're planning to... you know."

Jay did know. If she had clung to a single frayed thread of hope, the last strand parted under the guileless disclosure. "Yes, well—if you're planning to be here much longer, we're going to have to work out some sort of schedule."

Teddy? Good Lord, she actually called him Teddy?

Jay clumped down the back stairs in time to hear the front doorbell peal. Grabbing her purse, she ran through the house to take delivery of her supper. Not that she felt like eating now, but since she'd ordered the thing, she was obligated to pay for it.

Thad came down the front stairs just as she reached the foyer. "Were you expecting someone?"

"Yes," she snapped, concentrating on digging out her wallet.

"Me, too." He eyed her cautiously. "Look, about the hot water— Cyn told me there was a problem. I'm sorry. I should have thought to warn her to go easy."

He looked tired and harassed. His glasses were shoved up on top of his head, and he looked as if he hadn't slept all night.

Which was probably true, she thought with a sharp ache in the region of her heart that she preferred to think of as indigestion.

The doorbell sounded again and they both reached for it.

"Pizza delivery!" the boy sang out.

Their hands collided on the knob and they turned and frowned at one another. "Did you—?" Thad began.

"I ordered—" Jay said at the same time.

"Blanchard, one large with anchovies and green olives, twelve bucks even."

Thad handed over a fistful of bills, shut the door and laid the box on the hall table. "Jay, wait a minute," he said, sounding harried.

She had already turned away, feeling angry, embarrassed and hurt, telling herself it was only because of the pizza mix-up.

"Jay, wait a minute, will you?" He followed her through the house. "Look, about Cynthia—"

"Goodness, you don't owe me any explanations. You leased the entire second floor. It's none of my business how many guests you take in, but if there are going to be many more, we'll have to work out something about the hot water. I was told a forty-gallon heater is perfectly adequate for the average family, and since there are usually no more than two people—"

"I'll handle it."

She went to move past him, but he reached out and caught her arm, forcing her to meet his eyes. "Jay—I couldn't turn her away. She—"

"Thad, it's perfectly all right. You don't have to explain." If she'd been on a leaky life raft watching her whole dull existence flash before her eyes, she couldn't have felt more miserable.

"It's just that she depends on me. God knows why—Cyn's younger than you are, and she's already been through three husbands, but for some reason, I've always represented security to her."

"That's perfectly natural." Her smile was a brilliant work of art. "You're that kind of man. Reassuring, I mean."

He looked stunned. "God, is that what you think of me?"

She thought he was strong and caring and sexy and wonderful and the world's biggest fool. Not that she had any intention of telling him so. "Just warn her to go easy on the hot water, will you?"

"Jay, listen—" When a burst of loud music from the second floor interrupted, he glared at the ceiling. "I'll take care of that, too, while I'm at it."

"No problem," Jay assured him airily, still hanging on to her smile. "I'll be out in the studio all day tomorrow, and tomorrow night I'll probably go out." If she had to sit through an all-night movie by herself, she would do it.

"Look, it won't be for long. Cyn's just trying to hold it together until the wedding. After that, she'll be okay."

"The . . . wedding?"

"Wednesday. In Atlanta. And if I have to carry her every step of the way on my back, I intend to deliver her—"

The doorbell pealed again, and Jay shoved past him. Saved by the bell, she thought, fighting to hang on to her composure.

She swallowed hard and blinked her eyes several times. Oh, for heaven's sake, you'd think she was living in the Dark Ages! So she'd slept with a man. Big deal! It happened all the time. It was called a one-night stand, and just because she'd mistaken it for something else was no cause to throw herself on a funeral pyre.

"Pizza delivery!" The bell pealed again. Jay fixed another smile on her face, conscious of the fact that Thad was still standing where she'd left him, staring a hole between her shoulder blades.

"Goodness, it's about time," she said cheerfully. "I'm starving."

By midmorning she had everything arranged to suit her. Jars of brushes, racks of paper, stacks of blank canvases just waiting for her attention. She tried her easel in several positions and finally gave up looking for the perfect spot and started mixing fresh paint.

Thad and his redhead had driven off just after nine. Thad had looked grim. The redhead had looked petulant. Despite her age—and Jay thought he must have been mistaken about that—she'd been wearing a micromini skirt with a sheer camisole top, her ears studded with enough metal to plate a battleship. Cyn. That was what he'd called her. Probably spelled with an *S,* Jay thought snidely. At any rate, little Sin-Cyn looked like the type who'd sooner put a ring through a man's nose than on his finger.

Jay told herself she was being spiteful. Considering her own track record, both marriagewise and fashionwise, she was certainly in no position to talk.

She stared at her palette and then stared at her canvas. Touching the tip of her brush in white, she trailed it raggedly on a diagonal course across her canvas, then smudged it in several places with her thumb.

Sighing, she turned the canvas upside down on the easel. It wasn't working. It simply wasn't working....

And anyway, you'd think a man Thad's age would have better judgment. The little bimbo was going to make him miserable. What on earth could they have in common?

Sex?

Jay scooped up a blob of raw umber with her painting knife and jabbed it onto the canvas, obliterating an area of carefully detailed trees. She didn't want to think about sex. For Thad's sake, she hoped they had more going for them than that, although goodness knows, with Thad, sex was—

Well. At any rate, she hoped there was a functioning brain hidden under all that Clairol and Revlon. She knew from experience just how painful it was to watch your dreams erode away until there was nothing left of the illusion you'd fallen in love with.

Seventeen years ago she'd fallen head over heels for a charming scamp who had lived from whim to whim.

The trouble was, Ronnie's whims had never lasted very long. Jay knew. She'd been one of them. He had spent money as if it were water—mostly her money, and usually on himself—and then blamed her when it was all gone.

To her chagrin, Jay realized that she might have fallen into the same trap all over again if it hadn't been for Thad. He was a totally different species from Ronnie. And from Mike Weems.

Maybe his Cyn was more sensible than she looked. Jay knew for a fact how dangerous it was to judge a person by looks alone. At the age of twenty, she hadn't yet learned the truth of all those old clichés. That beauty was only skin-deep. That all that glittered was not gold.

Was it possible that Thad's lofty education had a few gaps in it? Should she try to save him from a life of heartache and disillusionment?

"Who're you kidding, Turner?" she grumbled, jerking the canvas off the easel. "You just want him for yourself."

Damn right she did! And she was just mean enough and selfish enough to go after what she wanted.

It was midafternoon when she heard Thad's car drive in. One quick glance in the kitchen mirror reassured her that her hair was still more or less in place and that her eye shadow and rouge didn't make her look like a Barnum and Bailey reject. Not quite.

Picking up the tray of lemonade, cookies and wafer sandwiches made with her fake smoked salmon dip, she hurried into the front parlor. "Oh, hi. Would either of you care for something cold to drink?" she asked, trying to sound as if she hadn't spent hours in the kitchen squeezing and mixing and baking.

"A cold beer would be—" the redhead began, when Thad narrowed his eyes at her. "I mean, whatever you've got in the pitcher looks good. Hey, thanks a bunch, Ms. Turner." She flopped down onto the love seat and kicked off her shoes. She was wearing a different outfit than the one she'd worn when she'd left. This one was marginally more respectable.

"Hey, I'm going to call you Jay, okay? Oh, wow, this is good!" She bit into a pecan sandy, scattering crumbs down her generous bosom, and brushed them off onto the floor. "Jeez, my feet hurt! We shopped until Teddy swore he wouldn't move another inch, but you ought to see what I got. Teddy, go get my loot and bring it in. I want to show it to Jay."

She's going to drive him wild. I give it three days, tops.

With a guileless look that belied the heavy makeup and the baggy eyes and the tight, flashy clothes, Cyn reached for another cookie. "Teddy says for a fourth wedding, I shouldn't wear white, but wait'll you see what I picked out, Jay. It's cotton, but it's got all this lace and stuff, and when I've got a tan, which I'm gonna start on tomorrow, I look terrific in white." She called after Thad, who was halfway out the door, his shoulders sagging. "Teddy, did you remember to make me an appointment at the tanning place? I want twenty minutes tomorrow and thirty on Tuesday, with a facial, a leg wax, a shampoo and set and a manicure. The works, okay?"

She'll kill him, Jay thought dejectedly. Or he'll kill her.

"Teddy's giving me all this great stuff as a wedding present. Isn't he sweet?"

Teddy was sweet. He was also the world's greatest fool. But if he loved her—if he truly loved her, and she loved him the way he deserved to be loved—Jay grudgingly wished them both well.

That night, she got out the newspaper, folded it to the personals column and carried it out onto the front porch. She had to have something to keep her from thinking, and painting wasn't going to do the job. That first ad had certainly taken her mind off her problems. For a few days at least. Actually, it hadn't been all bad. Sam had been sweet. Bob had been nice, but not her cup of tea. As for Mike...

Oh, well—two out of three wasn't bad. And this time she'd do the picking.

In the dim glow of the yellow porch light, she circled several of the most promising ads. The ones that sounded as if they might be mature and serious, strong and gentle. She underlined the ones who stated they were looking for someone with a sense of humor and X'ed out the ones who specified slender, not because she wasn't, but because she was looking for someone to whom looks were not the most important qualification.

The trouble was, she wasn't really looking for anyone. She'd already found the man she wanted, only he'd found someone else first. Leaving the paper in the cane rocker, she wandered over to the rail and twisted off a tendril of wisteria that was headed up the downspout.

One of these days she was going to have to get serious about her yard work. Only somehow, it no longer seemed to matter. What good was a home and a yard with no one to share it with?

"Balderdash," she muttered, and then, remembering where she'd last heard the word, she burst into tears and hurried inside.

By Wednesday morning, Cyn was several shades tanner. Surrounded by a stack of expensive new luggage, she looked radiant and as bridelike as a woman can look wearing high-heeled metallic fuchsia sandals, fuchsia leggings and a voluminous top of orange, pink and magenta chiffon.

Jay, on her way to school, met her at the foot of the stairs just as Thad came hurrying down, looking anything but groomlike. "Cyn, you're not wearing that rig to Atlanta."

"I always fly in tights. They keep my ankles from swelling. I think I look great in tights, don't you, Jay?"

"Wonderful color, too," Jay added.

"So *there!*"

Amused at the childish taunt, Jay kept on going. She'd had several days to come to terms with the situation and she was going to be all right. She'd be just fine as long as they didn't expect to honeymoon on her second floor.

"Jay, wait a minute, will you?" Grabbing the two largest bags, Thad hurried after her, looking as if he hadn't slept in weeks. It occurred to Jay that any man who would fly to Atlanta for his own wedding wearing baggy old khakis and a shirt that looked as if it had been slept in by a troop of Boy Scouts had no room to complain about his fiancée's costume.

He tossed the bags into the open trunk of his own car and turned to where Jay waited, a pasteboard smile tacked onto her face. "How long are you going to be away? Is there anything I can do for you while you're gone? I'll put your mail on—"

"Teddy, hurry up! I don't want to miss my plane!" Cyn caroled.

"Yeah, in a minute, honey," Thad called distractedly. "I'll be back by noon. I've got to go by my office first."

He'd be back by noon? Flying time to Atlanta was less than an hour. Make it two hours traveling time altogether, another hour for the wedding, and—

"Jay—don't plan anything for tonight, will you?"

"Ted-dy! Puh-*leeze!*"

"Yeah, yeah, coming, honey." He raked his fingers through his hair, leaving it standing on end. "Look, forget those ads you had circled. They all sound like losers to me, and besides—"

"Teddy," Cyn whined, scurrying up to hang on to his arm, "if you make me late for my wedding, I'll never ever forgive you!"

With a look that struck Jay as pleading, he turned to load the rest of the luggage into his car. Cyn was attached to his side like a hot pink barnacle by the time Jay backed out of her driveway.

My wedding? Not *our* wedding?

But Jay refused to hope. At the age of thirty-seven, after ten years of widowhood and a few notable lapses, she had finally grown up.

10

▬▶◀▬

Jay had appointments with three parents, a counselor and one especially gifted student scheduled for Wednesday. By day's end, she couldn't have said if her life depended on it what had transpired at any of the meetings. She only trusted she'd got through them without letting anyone down—including herself.

She hurried by the room where they had hung the year's-end exhibit, took one last look, suggested a minor change and left.

Don't make any plans for tonight, he'd said. Why not? Had he made plans—plans that included her?

My wedding, Cyn had said. Not *our* wedding, but *my* wedding.

Oh, great snakes alive, she'd be lucky if she didn't drive into a wall before she got home.

Thad's car was in the driveway when she pulled in. She half expected him to be waiting on the front porch for her, the way he had the first few days after she'd fallen off the ladder. With a quick glance to be sure he wasn't around, she dug into her shoulder bag and found her old compact, a lipstick and comb. Studying her image in the powdery mirror a moment later, she decided that it wasn't much of an improvement; however, it was the best she could do with the tools at hand. Looks weren't everything.

Which was all very well as long as you knew you had them.

The first thing she noticed was the flowers. They were everywhere. An enormous vase of jonquils and iris on the hall table. Three vases of daisies in the front parlor—yellow, pink and white. Roses and wild clematis in the silverplated ice bucket C.A. had given her for a wedding gift in the sitting room—and Thad in the kitchen, jamming a huge bunch of tulips and honeysuckle into a fruit jar.

"I ran out of vases."

Jay dropped down onto a chair. For no reason at all, she felt like weeping again. "Where on earth— Why?"

"Curb market. I got peaches, too. They're in the pantry."

"Thad, you don't owe me anything, for heaven's sake. If this is for the hot water and the—"

"It's for me." His big, square hands, clumsily arranging tulips while honeysuckle trailed around his muscular forearms, were so beautiful, it hurt. He had changed clothes since this morning. His khakis were neatly creased, his shirt, although open at the neck, with the sleeves turned up, was tucked in, and showed evidence of a recent encounter with an iron.

"No, what I mean is, it's for you. From me. Not for anything in particular, but because I wanted to give you something and I didn't know what you'd like."

"I like flowers. And peaches. They're beautiful, Thad, but you don't need to give me things. I don't understand," she said helplessly.

"I figured that might be the case. I should have explained before, but I've been walking on eggshells, wanting so damned bad to pull it off..."

Jay eased off her shoes. Her face felt sticky from the heat, and she'd put on too much lipstick. She wished she'd had a chance to shower before he came down. To shower and change into something elegant and feminine and slather herself in scented body lotion and do her nails and her hair. "Is that coffee I smell?"

He shoved the jar of flowers to the center of the table and took down two mugs. "I made fresh. Picked it up on the way from the airport at that coffee and wine place. Colombia excelsior."

"Would it keep long enough for me to jump under the shower? I've been sealing up cans of powdered pigment today, and I feel like I've been through a dust storm."

She made her escape, feeling as if she were seeing everything in a mirror. Sometimes when she was having trouble pulling a composition together, she held her canvas up to a mirror. It was a strange experience. Everything was the same, only different. If there was something out of kilter, it tended to jump out.

So what was wrong, she asked herself as she adjusted the temperature and stepped under the spray, with the picture she'd seen when she'd walked through her front door?

Nothing she could put her finger on, yet something was definitely different.

She lathered, rinsed and dried herself in record time. The body lotion would have to wait. She was reaching for her caftan when Thad called through the door. "You've got a phone call. Someone named Sue wants to know if you're up for Hungarian tonight. Says she got a raise and it's her treat."

Hearing his voice on the other side of the door when her caftan was twisted around her still damp shoulders, Jay panicked. Trying to tug the loose garment down over her hips, she knocked over the jar of bath salts, which struck the edge of the tub and spilled all over the floor.

Stepping in the stuff with her bare feet was no big thrill, either. "Tell her—tell her I'll call back!"

"Hey, are you all right in there?"

"No, I'm—yes, of course I'm all right, I'm just being my usual klutzy self." She sat on the edge of the tub and tried to dust the blue granules off the bottoms of her feet, but the towel was damp and so was she, and everything stuck, so groaning, she flung it to the floor.

"Stand by, I'm coming in," Thad said, and before she could yank her skirt down over her knees, he had opened the door. "What the devil is that blue stuff all over the floor?"

"English Garden with aloe—what does it look like?" she snapped. Her brother had once told her that when she set out to make a fool of herself, she did a really first-rate job of it.

"Sit tight, I'll get a broom and dustpan."

She didn't want him to get a broom and dustpan. She wanted him to sweep her up in his arms and carry her off somewhere where there were no classes full of kids who would rather be anywhere else in the world, no houses that needed rewiring and reroofing—no shrubbery that threatened to take over Carrboro, Chapel Hill and half of Orange County and no blue gunk all over her bathroom floor.

"Lift 'em," he said, and lift 'em she did. Perched on the edge of her claw-footed bathtub, Jay watched while Thaddeus Blanchard, visiting lecturer in the anthropology department of the oldest state-supported university in the country cleaned up her bathroom floor and hung her towel neatly over the shower rod.

Jay had dreamed of love. She'd dreamed of romance, more times than was good for her in the past few weeks. None of her dreams had included a scene like this.

"Thank you," she said because she couldn't think of anything to say that wouldn't alarm him.

Would you mind taking off your clothes and letting me see if your body is really as magnificent as I remember?

Would you mind holding me in your arms until I forget that life is real, life is earnest and the only thing kissing frogs gets you is a mouthful of warts?

"It's still sticky. Better let me carry you," Thad said, and before she could argue, he swung her up into his arms.

His face was too close to hers. She could feel his breath stirring the damp tendrils of hair on her neck, and the sensation acted like a tourniquet on her lungs.

"Jay?" he asked, his voice a deep, soft rumble of sound. "Are you too tired?"

"Too tired?"

"From work. From being out all day."

"From work?" His eyes were the color of black-strap molasses, full of mysterious shadows and glinty little lights.

"Because if you're not..."

"If I'm not?" she breathed. There was a look on his face that she had never before seen on any man's face. Soul to soul. Heart to heart. A look so fragile, she was afraid she might wake up any moment and realize she had dreamed it all.

"If you're not, I thought maybe we could go upstairs and, uh—talk?"

"Talk?" So much for soul to soul, heart to heart and fragile. She took control of her wits and said, "We can talk over coffee. In the kitchen. I need to call Sue back and tell her—"

"I already told her."

"What?"

"That you had other plans."

"I do?" There was a crazy sort of dialogue going on in here, and it had nothing to do with the words being spoken.

"We got off the track a few days ago. I wasn't expecting Cyn to show up like that. It couldn't have happened at a worse time." A bleak smile deepened the grooves in his cheeks. Jay wanted to touch them, to kiss them, to smooth the furrows between his winged brows.

Instead, she said in her firm, back-to-work voice, "You might as well put me down before you drop me, Thad. Now. If you'll pour the coffee, I'll join you as soon as I check in with Sue."

"I'm sorry if I spoke out of turn. Maybe you can catch her before she makes other arrangements."

He sounded so disheartened that she shrugged and pulled out a kitchen chair instead. "It'll wait. All right, what did you want to talk about? If it's about your lease—"

"Dammit, Jay, what is it with you? I could have sworn it meant something to you—what we had. What we did—the other night."

She felt as if she'd been out in the sun too long. Her cheeks felt hot against her cool palms as she struggled against the hope that was beginning to rise again inside her. "If you mean what I think you mean, then yes."

"Yes? What kind of answer is that?"

"I don't know. You haven't asked me a question yet."

"Yeah, well, I intend to, and I'll just take that answer in advance, but first you'd better know about Cyn."

Jay braced herself. Thad poured coffee, and she noticed that his hands were not quite steady. He fixed hers the way she liked it and stirred it until she gently removed the mug from his hands. "About Cyn?" she prompted.

"Oh. Right. Cyn." He looked embarrassed. Or at least as embarrassed as a big, successful man who was too self-confident to worry about the opinions of others could look. "You knew we were once married," he said. She hadn't, but she'd begun to wonder. "We were both too young to know better. For her it was a way out of a lousy situation at home. For me—" He grinned ruefully, and Jay decided to let him tell it—whatever *it* was—in his own way. "You wouldn't believe how green I was. She told me I was her first, and I believed her. Regardless of what you've heard, a guy can't always tell. Anyhow, I liked the idea of marriage. Home. Family. Figured we might as well go for it."

He twiddled with the spoon, tracing the design with his fingertip. "Neither of us was much good at it, as it turned out. Cyn was a party girl, any party—anytime. Me, I just wanted to settle down and start building a future. We split and went our own ways. Cyn headed west. I went back to school. Paid for it with a gambling scholarship, you might say. Anyhow, we kept in touch over the years. You don't just stop worrying about someone you've cared for, even when you've long since stopped caring that way.''

''You said she'd been through a couple of husbands,'' Jay reminded him. It hurt to see such a strong man made so very vulnerable. She had a feeling he needed to talk even more than she needed to listen. Unlike some of the men she had met lately, Thad didn't talk about himself. Too much reticence was worse than not enough.

''She married twice after we split. They were both losers, but she couldn't see it. Cyn had a problem with alcohol that started when she was in high school, and that didn't help matters. Anyway, I got her into a clinic about ten years ago, and once she dried out she managed to stay on the wagon until her second marriage went under. After that, it got to be a pattern. Binge, dry out and binge again. The last time I sent her money she used it for a fling in the Bahamas and ended up in a detox center in Miami. From then on I refused to get involved, until she turned up on my doorstep.''

''I didn't know—I didn't realize...''

''She wasn't drinking here. That's why she came. She knew I'd keep her straight until she got on the plane to Atlanta. Her tractor salesman met her on the other end, and from now on she's his problem.'' He shook his head, staring down at his untouched mug.

"I hope it works out. Cyn's got a lot to offer some man if she can only get a grip on her problems."

Jay's heart sank. "You?"

He looked startled. "You mean do I still want her? No way! I've found what I've been looking for. Didn't you know? Haven't I made it clear?"

Slowly she shook her head. "Made what clear?" In her heart she knew, but she was afraid to let herself hope.

Rising to his full towering height, Thad held out his hand. "I thought you knew. If I've got to start all over again, I'd just as soon do it somewhere more comfortable." So saying, he grabbed the jar of tulips and honeysuckle off the table, took her hand in his other hand and led her toward the back stairs.

Several hours later they lay side by side in his big bed, Jay's head on Thad's shoulder, both his arms around her. They had talked about his work and the dream of security that had made her hang on to a lovely old relic of a house against all odds. They had made love until they were both sated and then woke and made love again.

Yet neither of them had quite dared speak the words. Tempting fate. It was a dangerous thing to do.

"I've never had a real home," he confided. "Not one of the lasting kind. Funny... I've always liked things that are built to last. Occupational hazard, I guess."

"I grew up in the home my grandfather built. My family still lives there—those who haven't moved to their own homes. This house—" She waved a hand in the general direction of the ornate mantel above the closed-up fireplace, and Thad caught it and brought it to his lips to nibble her fingertips. "This was supposed to be our security. We were going to turn it into a bed and breakfast and raise a family here, but by the time we got through all the red tape of mortgages and insurance and everything that goes with buying a house, Ronnie had lost interest. I tried to pretend the dream was still real, but he went back to school for a while, and then he started talking about opening a gym, only by then, I'd stopped listening, and then he died. His heart."

"I'm sorry, sweetheart." Thad turned her in his arms so that she was lying against him, so close he could feel the beat of her heart. He told her he was sorry her dream hadn't worked out, and she told him she was sorry about Cyn, but she didn't mention the heart-deep loneliness she had sensed in him almost from the beginning. That was something she fully intended to change.

"Have you ever thought about traveling? You don't teach all year round, after all, and I know some wonderful landscapes just begging to be painted."

"Ohhhh…" He was slowly stroking the sole of her foot with his toes, sending shivers up the lazy length of her legs. "The house—how could I leave it?"

"Have you ever considered leasing out the whole thing? With the equity you've already built up, the house would pay for itself and be waiting here for us when we got tired of traveling."

"We?"

Tilting her head up to his, Thad searched her eyes, seeking the assurance she couldn't quite bring herself to put into words. Daring the fate they were both almost afraid to tempt. "If you'll have me. There's probably a better way to do this, sweetheart, but as you might've noticed, my drawing room manners are a little rough."

Laughter gurgled in her voice. "But your bedroom manners are exemplary, Dr. Blanchard."

"Yeah ... they're not bad, are they?" He grinned, but then he fell serious. "Jay, if love means anything, then you've got it."

"Love means everything," she whispered. He kissed her then, and the kiss quickly ignited. Rolling over onto his back, Thad lifted her onto his eager body, wordlessly encouraging the creative streak of sheer sexuality he had earlier uncovered, to their mutual delight.

"Say it," he urged as he guided her into the languorous dance of love.

"Say what?" Her eyes half closed, she trailed her fingertips over his sensitive male nipples...and lower.

Thad caught her hands and held them away, his face flushed with the strain of control. "Say it."

"For such a quiet man, you certainly do like to talk."

Suddenly their positions were reversed. Lying on her back, her hair in a dark silken tangle across her face, Jay laughed until tears came to her eyes while Thad knelt over her, holding her captive.

"If you want to finish this waltz, madam, you'll tell me what I want to hear," he growled, and she laughed all the harder.

"There aren't any words," she whispered when she could speak again. "They've all been used so many times on silly little things. But if it's words you want, then it's words you'll have," and she pulled his head down and whispered in his ear.

"*Yes!*" he said quietly, but with great feeling a moment later.

And the waltz continued.

* * * * *